Too Many Clues

"Mr. Webb," Sergeant Holliman said, "can you name me one particular thing about this case which is odder than anything else?"

"One of the oddest things is that there are too many clues," Webb said. "You might say that trying to solve this case is like trying to hear the symphony hidden amongst the notes a child pounds on the piano. Therefore, eliminate the extraneous or the misleading, and it will be perfectly clear."

"Then you can solve the case?" Holliman asked.

"Forgive the musical allusion," Webb said, "but I think I'm beginning to hear the melody."

MUSIC TO MURDER BY

VERNON HINKLE

LEISURE BOOKS ≈ NEW YORK CITY

*This book is for
Larry Mowers
who probably could have solved
this mystery faster.*

A LEISURE BOOK

Published by

Dorchester Publishing Co., Inc.
6 East 39th Street
New York, NY 10016

Copyright ©MCMLXXVIII by Vernon Hinkle

All rights reserved. No part of this book may be reproduced or transmitted in any form or by any electronic or mechanical means, including photocopying, recording, or by any information storage and retrieval system, without the written permission of the Publisher, except where permitted by law.

Printed in the United States of America

MUSIC TO MURDER BY

Chapter I

On no previous Thursday since we began the ritual had Dr. Sterne and I enjoyed such an evening. An unusually sensitive performance of *Bolero* (unannounced, unexpected) was followed by a superb dinner in an uncrowded restaurant which provided conscientious service. Despite the heat of this humid August night, the air conditioning was not too cold, neither in Symphony Hall nor in the restaurant. For once, the compatibility I shared with my companion became harmonious with our surroundings, everything going as we would have wished. It was a perfect evening. Yes, everything about it pointed to disaster.

I could not be certain if Sterne sensed this as I did, or if I only projected my own uneasiness onto him. More than usual his fingers seemed to unconsciously probe for his receding hairline. And his features became more cherubic, which was his polite manner of masking apprehension. Indeed, so unused were we to perfection that we became uncomfortable in its presence, suspecting it was a calm designed to entice one to walk innocently into an unexpected and terrible storm.

In fact, it had been during a storm that Dr. Sterne first revealed to me the secret of the universe. We were caught in a downpour, and were attempting to dash to our destination under the protection of available canopies and awnings. Invariably, we were foiled by masses of people who were doing the same. The difference was that they were all carrying umbrellas.

"It never fails," Sterne muttered. "When one is caught in a downpour and has no umbrella, all space beneath awnings will be occupied by people *with* umbrellas!"

"That sounds like a corollary to Murphy's Law," I said. "If anything can possibly go wrong, it will."

"Murphy didn't go far enough," Sterne growled. "If anything *cannot* possibly go wrong, it will!"

"Sterne's Law," I said.

"If you wish," he smiled.

It brought me some comfort to recall this incident during the thoughtful moment when Sterne was ruminating over how best to deal with our pleasant evening. Finally, he chose to ignore it and concentrate instead on the imperfections of the past.

"We both know that Bolero has been badly overplayed," he said as he reached for his wineglass.

"That plus its obvious sensuality makes it easily underrated," I nodded.

"Yes," he sighed. "If only conductors would take composers more seriously, who knows what treasures might be unearthed from the graveyard of popularity. Ravel has clearly indicated the proper tempo for *Bolero*, and that unrelenting tempo is what makes the work emotionally powerful. But Ravel himself was the only man to conduct it properly."

"Tonight's performance was close," I said in a transparent attempt to add a dark counterpoint to the present. "Just close enough to give one a sense of the power you mention."

"Yes," said Sterne with a trace of concern. "I feared for your health." He was referring to my chronic and medically elusive ailment which has asthmatic symptoms but can become so aggravated by emotional stress that, on more than one occasion, it has made me question my hold on life.

"Ah well," I joked, "I could not wish to go at a better time."

"Dear friend," chided Sterne, "think how inconvenient that would be for me."

"I only meant that going on the wings of song, as it were, might at least get me started in the proper direction."

At this point Sterne chuckled, a very rare occurence and somewhat inflating to my ego. Joking about my fluctuating health was my way of putting him at ease, but my past relationship with Sterne gave no precedent for such an uninhibited reaction. I allowed myself a safe ration of ecstasy.

"You know," he said, seeming to welcome my dark humor, "there may be more to your..." he paused, carefully finding the proper word..."more to your 'condition' than we suspect."

"How do you mean?"

"Well, it's quite selective, *isn't* it?" He gave the British rhetorical turn to the question. "That is to say, an attack might have occured because of tonight's performance, but would be out of the question while exerting yourself on the handball court."

I had long been aware of the dichotomy and could only shrug.

"Well," he smiled, "perhaps someday someone will appear with medical skill as well as a medical degree, and he will provide the logic behind it all. After all, a human contradiction is merely logic we have not yet learned to understand, is it not so? And now, if you are expecting your literary gentleman, it is time for us to finish our coffees."

He was referring to the arrival that evening of my good friend, Jerome Lamphere, whom I had not seen since I was last in New York almost a year previously. He was now visiting me to discuss his new novel. "Yes," I told Sterne, "Jerome has probably been waiting for my arrival. Would you care to join us?" I offered the amenity as I obediently raised my cup.

"If I were going to meet anyone for the first time, I

should prefer that he not be a stranger."

I anticipated this response, for it was one of Sterne's favorite expressions and one I had often used myself. Of course, like a true scholar, I always gave proper credit with "As my good friend Dr. Sterne is wont to say..." My good friend! It was a fact that I had several very close friends and practically no acquaintances. Some might call it snobbery, others—such as my friends—good taste. I called it prudence. Most of my friendships had grown comfortably over a period of years.

Dr. Sterne was no exception. For over a year I assisted him in his research at the music library where I am head librarian. The relationship was no more than that of one scholar to another.* Then one day Dr. Sterne approached my desk with special reverence.

"Mr. Webb," he said with a quiet air of importance, "I have just discovered seven new motets by Lorenzio."

"Good heavens!" I replied, "not seven *more!*"

After that we began to spend Thursday evenings together.

On this Thursday it was my turn to pay the check and Dr. Sterne the gratuity. Such simple understandings obviated vulgar and insincere scufflings.

"The full fifteen percent, I think," said Sterne counting out the tip. I agreed, for the service had been excellent. How my good friend Jerome would have laughed at this had he been able to arrive early enough to join us. He, putting himself in the waitress' shoes, so he thought, would tip fifteen percent in any case, and more if the service was excellent.

There was no rain as Sterne and I emerged from the restaurant. The Grey Ghost, my 1970 Oldsmobile, was not trapped by another double-parked. It started

---

*I'm afraid only other scholars will know what I mean by that.

promptly. No traffic lights turned red as we approached them. No motorist in the right lane took a left turn in front of us. Sterne ignored these things, but as he was alighting at his apartment building, he tried to convince me that he heard an ominous sound in the motor. He was clearly grasping at straws. The Grey Ghost was feeling friendly that evening, and there was no sound.

Perhaps, I thought as I continued homeward, this was the day we each live for, that one day when everything goes well. And then I shuddered, knowing that this optimistic thought was tempting the execution of Sterne's Law.

I tried turning my thoughts elsewhere, to my friend who would be waiting for me at home by now. He had himself been a corollary to Sterne's Law, something like "the most promising marriages will not work out." He had left his wife Doris, a seemingly ideal mate, about three years ago. At the same time he gave up a most desirable position as an instructor in a junior college near here. "My life is out of joint," he told me. "I married before I knew what I was doing. I got a nice, comfortable job that I would have welcomed thirty years from now. And now I'm finally pursuing a dream I should have gone after twenty years ago."

The dream, equally improbable, was to go to New York City and become a writer. Later he wrote me that even though he had ended up writing articles for fan magazines, he had found a peace he had never known in marriage. I offered further comfort by telling him that my own life had become so much simpler when I realized that there were some things that could never possibly be done. I suppose I had been referring to my own early and insane thoughts of marriage and/or teaching.

Then one day while trying on a suit in a clothing store, I looked at myself in a full-length mirror. The suit, which I could ill afford, hung on my small, wiry frame like moss on a tree branch. I knew that in a moment the salesman would tactfully suggest that I could be more properly fitted in the boys' department.

There I was with the shape of a boy, the few gray wisps of an elder statesman, and a great-grandfather's internal physical condition—too young to gracefully accept the contradictions and not old enough to be dignified as "a character." As I looked in that mirror and caught myself standing stiffly in some absurd attempt to fill out the suit, it made me laugh aloud.

"Well," suggested the salesman misinterpreting my reaction, "some men of your conservative stature prefer the tailoring and greater economy to be found in the boys' department."

I relaxed and smiled and allowed the suit to hang limply. In that instant, I accepted it all, everything I was and was not.

Now I was living in South Boston, my favorite part of my favorite city. I was the head librarian of one of Harvard's music libraries, a position suitable to my health and temperament. Good heavens, was I happy?!

I shuddered at the thought and purposefully drove through Boston's seediest area known appropriately as "the combat zone." Here was something to openly despise, this garish and flagrant exhibition of vice and corruption. Here were the cheap penny arcades, the brothels, the pornographic bookstores, the theatres with flashing marquees, suggestive titles starring obviously fictitious names. Well might they hide behind pseudonyms, these tarnished stars.

Of course, I expected to see all this, and I came to see it to add a note of reality to an evening that had been going too nicely for comfort. But then I saw something I did not expect. One marquee loudly proclaimed

IN PERSON-SUNDAY & MONDAY ONLY-PETER PIPER.

How could one of them have the audacity to appear in public? How did this relate to the protection of a counterfeit name? I had seen enough, I thought, and somewhat reassured proceeded homeward to South Boston.

As I drove up to Webb Manor (the glorified name for my humble abode), I saw a familiar auto parked outside. It was the BMW which belonged to a lady friend of Jerome's. When I visited him, it was his duty to protect it from being towed away by moving it daily from one side of the street to the other.* The auto's presence on my street was evidence that Jerome's newest relationship was still intact and had weathered the previous year. I say "weathered" because Martha had been Jerome's student, and it cannot be easy when there exists such a disparity in ages. Older men—Jerome was thirty-eight—are often so vulnerable to the promise of an eternal romance with perennial youth. And younger girls, with youthful resilience, are prepared to survive many such romances. We never spoke about it.

My spirits sank once more as, without effort, I found a parking place.

The key was where I always left it, behind a loose shingle.

I opened the front door leading onto the hallway and the staircase going up to two other apartments. I felt once more the pride of ownership. (Only one of the apartments, alas, was presently rented.) My own door

---

*A routine made necessary by alternate-side-of-the-street parking, a ritual which allows street cleaners, when they are not out on strike, to clean alternate curbs on alternate days and thereby more effectively keep New York streets from drowning in saliva and—excuse me—dog manure.

was at the end of the first floor hallway, and it was ajar.

When I entered the apartment the first things I noticed was Jerome's small duffel bag. The next things I saw were Jerome and his estranged wife Doris. They were in the bedroom. They were dead.

Chapter II

I should like to point out that the manner in which I ended the first chapter was an attempt to suggest the emotional content of the moment, the surprise, the shock, the acceptance. However well one is prepared for *general* disaster, he is seldom sufficiently prepared for any *specific* disaster. It was some self-protective shock that kept me from experiencing the horror—at least temporarily— and put me into that objective state which permits examination of any subject without emotional involvement.

The scene was gory—and, I probably should add, totally without sexual connotations. In the small apartment I have chosen for myself, the so-called "bedroom" is little more than an extension of the living room. It is merely where the bed happens to be, so let us immediately dispense with any lurid speculations. Both Jerome and his wife* were fully clothed.

Blood glistened in Doris' peroxide hair which some years ago she had changed from ordinary brown, perhaps, she thought, to help hold Jerome's interest in the early stages of marital dissolution. She was lying on the floor parallel to the foot of the bed. A gun was lying on the floor between her and the bed.

Jerome was sprawled the length of the bed, with his bent hand dangling over the foot, his fingers pointing toward the gun. There was blood shining wet all over his face and hair.

That, I believe, is enough. Entirely too much violence is

---

*Alas, I'm afraid I still think of her as such. They never had gotten around to the actual divorce, and now there was no need to.

depicted these days, and I have no wish to continue the precedent.

Once I absorbed the aforementioned details, I approached my former friends and searched for signs of life in their bodies. No, not the slightest spasm of a lung caused either of them to occupy any more nor less space from one unliving moment to the next. The only movement in the room was the slow trickle of blood down Doris' still-blonde hair.

I moved to the telephone in my living room (so-called) and automatically dialed the number of James O'Toole, no doubt an excellent policeman, though somewhat less successful on the handball courts. It was Mrs. O'Toole who answered.

"Hello, Sarah. This is Martin. Is James in?"

"You'd stand a better chance of finding him at just about any pub than you would here, Marty." Some day I must find the courage to ask her not to call me that.

"I see," I said noncommittally. "Do you know where he might be reached?"

"He told me, for what that's worth, that he was picking up some extra money for directing traffic at Fenway Park, Marty. Of course they'd all be gone from there by now, so... wait a minute, it's himself."

"Hello," said James, his voice drifting in as he took the receiver from his wife. "What's up, Martin me boy?" He insisted on living his impression of an Irish cop.

"James, could you come over here now?"

"There wouldn't be anything I'd like more. But a certain sense of commitment draws me to the hearth." Then I overheard him say away from the receiver, "Oh, hush up. I'm not goin' anywhere."

"I'm sorry I disturbed you at this hour, James."

"Don't be givin' it a second thought. I was just getting in anyway. Been out making the little girl's tuition, and then celebrating the success of same. Suppose I come over early in the morning and give you a ride to the library. We could talk it over then, whatever it is.

"Yes," I said. "But the problem probably requires immediate action. I'll call the precinct." I could not bring myself to be more specific over the phone. I suppose I spoke in a dazed tone of voice, for I was as stunned as if I had taken morphine.

There was a silence at the other end, and then James' voice, less cheery than before: "Is it trouble you're in then? I'll be there before you hang up the phone."

And he was true to his word, because after the click on the other end, I stood entranced with the receiver in my hand, oblivious to its complaint, as I contemplated some oddly shaped stains on the bedroom wallpaper, strange horizontal exclamation points.

I was just replacing the receiver in its cradle when James, resplendent in his uniform, came bursting in. "Jaisus!" was his comment. He stood stock still as though all life had been suspended, giving the viewer the opportunity of studying a single moment. James' ruddy Irish features grew ashen, accentuating by contrast his rusty red hair which blazed free-form high atop his head some six brawny feet from the ground.

The action resumed abruptly, and James jolted into the bedroom. "Good lord a'mighty! It's Dorie." And he began to weep.

He had met Doris about a year earlier at a dance where I had taken her to meet some of my friends, hoping I suppose that she would find some new romantic interest. It was a very Irish dance. In fact, it was sponsored by our local chapter of the Irish Republican Army of which I was a member.

Although he was not an official member, I had met James at my first IRA meeting. "To be an official member of this organization," he told me, "*and* an officer of the law might be regarded by both sides as a conflict of interest." But he was allowed to attend the meetings, and happily joined a few vocal exhibitionists in advocating a bloody revolution on the old sod. But like the others, James was more in danger of harming himself from pounding his fist on the table than he was of effecting any change in the old country.

I was a member only to add a note of sanity to it all. At my encouragement, all of the incendiary plots were ultimately drowned in pints of ale. Then James would weep, as he did now, as easily as he seemed to accept the banality of being Irish and a policeman.

This time his weeping took the form of great convulsions which were soon spent. He wiped his eyes with his sleeve in a kind of mime gesture which changed his face from sorrowful to solemn. He fixed me with his green-eyed stare and asked me huskily, "Have you got anything to drink?"

Why hadn't I thought of this? I started toward the kitchen (an actual room), but he stopped me and said, "No, you mustn't touch anything. Don't move. I'll get it." He showed me his white gloved hands and disappeared into the kitchen, soon returning with one very large drink of my favorite Jameson's Whiskey. I was perplexed.

"I'm in uniform," he explained, then took a healthy gulp from the glass and handed it to me. "There are stains in the sink," he told me. "Maybe blood." He began to make notes in a notebook he carried. Without looking up, he asked me, "Now tell me true, Martin, can you prove that you had nothing to do with this?"

"Prove it?"

"It isn't always the guilty they're hanging. Can you prove you weren't here when it happened?"

I told him that I had been with Dr. Sterne all evening,

that when I returned I saw the horrid scene, and then I called him.

"What did you touch?" he asked me, writing.

I thought a bit, carefully retracing it in my own mind. "The latch key, the doorknobs and the telephone."

He nodded and dialed the police. "When they get here," he said, "tell them the truth."

After he had summoned the police, he removed the gun from his holster and asked me for the keys to the upstairs apartments. "He may still be here," he said. I shuddered at the thought. He went bounding up the stairs and returned alone. At his suggestion we took our drink to the stoop outside and waited there.

"Can you make it through the rest of the evening?" he asked.

"With the help of God and Jameson's Whiskey," I said raising the latter in a toast to the Former. "Confusion to our enemies," I added for good measure.

There was a pause, and then he asked me, "Where's your tenant this evening? Mrs. Hall?"

"She's visiting her sister until Monday," I told him, and he wrote it down. "It's a blessing for her not to be here. She so hates any kind of disturbance."

Our peace was short-lived. Soon a police car drove quietly up to the curb and stopped. There emerged a tall man in a neatly pressed suit. He nodded to us, motioned us to sit still, then pivoted suddenly to survey the buildings across the street. Then he leaned into the car and said something. A uniformed officer got out, went across the street and rang the Donahue's doorbell. In the meantime, another plain-clothes man appeared with a pad and pencil. The two men approached us.

"I'm Sergeant Holliman," the tall man told me as we shook hands. "How can you be so calm?" he asked in a friendly manner. I was surprised and could find nothing to say. "Never mind," he reassured me, "everyone reacts differently." He nodded to O'Toole who opened the door. Then he shoved his hands deeply in his pockets and went inside, followed by the other man with the pad and pencil.

James gave me a puzzled look. "Calm?"

I thought a moment. "Perhaps when he shook my hand, he saw that I wasn't trembling and that my palm was dry."

James shook his head in admiration, and then we went into the hallway. Once there, we paused. Inside my apartment, Sergeant Holliman seemed to be dictating to his companion. "Stains on the wall, north to south, as though bleeding body swung toward bed. Stain on gun butt. Apparently weapon which clubbed woman. Man shot in temple, angle uncertain. Check lint on man's clothing."

He's a——to work for," James whispered, "but he knows what he's doing."

After a considerable time, Holliman and the other man reappeared. Holliman gestured for us to follow him outside. When we got there, there was a police van parked behind the patrol car. Holliman signaled to the vehicles, and several men emerged carrying cameras, tripods, cases and various paraphernalia. They moved into the house with blustering professionalism.

"Make sure they get it all the first time," Holliman said to his partner who nodded and followed them inside.

Holliman asked me to wait on the stoop and James to accompany him. They went out into the street where they were joined by the policeman who came out of the Donahue house carrying a pad and pencil. Referring to his pad, he made checkmarks on it as he reported to Holliman. Then James opened his pad and referred to his notes. "No signs of rigor mortis," I heard him report.

"In this heat?" Holliman asked him. "What did you

expect?" James nodded. Holliman shook his head, then approached me smiling, his face flashing light as flashbulbs popped behind my windows. "Mr. Webb," he said, "I understand that this Jerome Lamphere came here from New York City this evening."

"Yes."

"Alone?"

"I believe so."

"His wife didn't accompany him?"

"I don't think so. They had not been together for three years."

"How did he arrive? By plane?"

"No, I believe he drove a car." I pointed to the BMW. "That one."

Holliman again shoved his hands deeply in his pocket. He returned to the road and examined the car without touching it. "And Mrs. Lamphere?" he asked. "How might she have arrived?"

"She drove a green Volkswagen," I said. "But I don't see it here on the street."

James nodded toward the BMW from the sidewalk. "It's in need of a bath," he said.

"Very interesting," said Holliman from the street. "This side, the driver's side, looks perfectly clean."

Chapter III

Once again, Holliman conferred with James beyond earshot. As he did so, I scanned the street from my vantage point on the stoop. I still saw no green Volkswagen. Then how *did* Doris arrive? Or even more important, why was she here in the first place?

Frequently she would come into Boston from her small cottage in the nearby town of Wessex. We would have dinner together or see a play. However, she never arrived on a Thursday because she well knew this was my evening with Dr. Sterne. And it is unlikely she would have arrived on this *particular* Thursday since she had been told that her husband would be spending the weekend with me. She would not want to see him. She would want to avoid any residue of bitterness in herself or, because she was procrastinating about the divorce, any frustration in him.

Perhaps I was heard mumbling to myself, for James approached me with exceptional concern and placed a gentle hand on my shoulder.

"Martin?" he asked as though to inquire if anyone was at home, "Sergeant Holliman has a number of questions he would like to ask you. But we both think it best if you and I called it a night and just left his men in charge here. So you're to come home with me for the night. Mary being away at school, you can have her room. Then if you feel up to it, we'll drop by the station in the morning."

I agreed to go along with whatever he and the sergeant thought best.

When we arrived at the O'Toole home we were accosted by Sarah, her nostrils flaring with anger as they picked up the scent of whiskey on our breaths. But a look from her husband silenced her, and I was whisked into their daughter's room where the indomitable Sarah mobilized into a flurry of activity as she tossed stuffed animals off the bed.

"This isn't exactly a man's room, Marty, but I guess once you close your eyes it won't make any difference. There's a new mattress on the bed, anyway, and the sheets are clean."

James soon arrived at the doorway with a glass in hand. "We're short on glasses, Martin, my boy. And, unfortunately, this one is full of whiskey, so you'll have to dispose of the contents before you brush your teeth." A toothbrush was stuck in the glass like a swizzle stick.

"If there's anything you're needin' just give a holler," said Sarah as James ushered her out of the room. I could hear them speaking in hushed tones as they went down the stairs.

I undressed and sat on the edge of the bed, for only a moment it seemed, but when I next looked at my glass it was empty and seemed to be spinning in my hand. I remember the precision with which I placed the empty glass and the unused toothbrush on the bedside table, found my favorite station on the clock-radio and set it for my usual time of awakening. These rituals attended to, I fell back onto the bed.

For a moment I was helpless. The whiskey had flushed away my protective covering, and I lay staring up at the emotional reality of the evening. I was suddenly overcome by grief and convulsed with tears, tears which shook me until I felt I would quite literally fall to pieces. It turned into an attack, my first in weeks. It came surging up from the bottom of the lungs and exploded out in a cough which emptied me of air. This done, my trachea constricted to keep air from flowing back. The eerie, discordant music of my wheezing echoed between my ears. If I had not been drunk, the fight might well have killed me. But as it was, such a corporeal breakup was mercifully postponed as I either fainted or fell asleep.

There were dreams, I know. I always dream. Sleep and dreams have probably saved my life on more than one occasion. Some nights I would be awake, it seemed endlessly, fighting a suffocating attack until I fell unconscious onto the bed, and awoke a day or two later, momentarily cured.*

During one of these sleeps I dreamt of being on a mountain top, high above the pollution line. The air was pure and invigorating. I shared it only with a flock of bluebirds. I remember thinking, "So this is where they've gone!"

Ah, precious sleep and dreams! While in college, I discovered another application. There was a course in which I never took notes, never consciously listened. I never studied until two days before the final and only exam. Then I sat up studying into the wee hours, not seeming to absorb any information, but forcing myself into the ritual atonement, pushing myself mercilessly until I collapsed and slept. When I awoke, I knew everything I needed to pass the exam. It all came to me in a dream.**

---

*A psychologist friend has theorized that I acquired an ability, in crisis, to maneuver my way to the "survival level," that mental state which, supposedly, permits humans to do super-human things. She told me of elderly ladies lifting automobiles off trapped children and so forth.

**This recalls two things to mind. (1) Several composers and performers had developed mental capabilities which contributed to their musical superiority. Some seemed to create in a semi-hypnotic state which eliminated all but the best choices, making them geniuses in a life which, by accident or design, offered an infinity of possibilities in any given situation. (2) Stern's Law simplified life by merely accepting the worst as the only possibility and circumvented semi-hypnosis (unless you wish to argue that anyone who saw life in eternal negatives was, in fact, hypnotized by virtue of his obsession).

However, I remembered very little of my dreams on the fateful evening I found my friends dead.

When I awoke, the radio was playing Mozart's *Quintet in D Major*, a soothing and welcome piece. Apparently, the music had filtered into my dream, and it recalled an image of my late friend, Jerome, sitting in my living room, reading aloud from a manuscript and drinking whiskey from a bottle. That was all.

Despite the music, I was afraid to move for fear of reviving the attack of last evening.

A small white telephone was near at hand, but I could not even make the effort necessary to dial it and inform Miss Pinkham (my assistant at the library, a lovely woman) that I would be absent from my duties, even though I knew she would be calling me soon, and that the loud jangle of the telephone (certainly no fault of Miss Pinkham's) would sacriligiously impose itself back at the scene of carnage.

Faced with that memory, my objective mind once again took me in its cold, comforting hands. And it was then that I began to wonder if those streaks of blood could be removed from wallpaper. Had I unwittingly invoked Sterne's Law when only two months ago I had newly papered my bedroom? There were books on the subject of removing stains, I seemed to recall. I must look one up. But I realized it might be some time before I could attend to this particular detail, there being so many others with greater priority.

Yes, let us attend to all the details one by one. Let us sort things out, put each thing in its proper place, lay each to rest.

I got up, made the bed and carefully replaced the stuffed animals exactly as they had been the night before. Then I sat down on the bed, listened to the Mozart and waited to be summoned to breakfast. I was very hungry.

Chapter IV

It was my first time in a police station, and I was somewhat awed by the experience.

It was going to be another warm day, and the building seemed grimly awaiting the worst. James led me past the implacable brick facade, through cheerless green hallways and into what appeared to be the detectives' room where tobacco-stale air apathetically contemplated the open windows. Several detectives hunched over desks, typewriters and telephones as though they were all bracing themselves for another hot day. The very walls seemed ready to perspire.

I recognized two of the detectives as having been at my apartment with Holliman the night before, but Holliman was not to be seen. James shifted nervously from one foot to the other.

"I'll have to leave you, Martin, if that's all right," he said. "I have to go on duty."

Before I could assent we were interrupted by a fat pipe smoker at the desk nearest me. He was hanging up the telephone as he told James, "Not today, O'Toole. The message is for you to wait here."

"Thanks," said James.

"I don't know about that," said the detective who turned his attention to some papers on his desk.

James was clearly nervous.

A plump, elderly lady came busily muttering by. "Stinks!" she said. "This place stinks! Needs a good old airing out, it does." She stopped abruptly when she saw me. "Ah, Mr. Webb, God love you! I've tried to reach you, but of course you weren't at home."

"Sad times, Mrs. Donahue," I said. "What brings you to this place?"

"I wanted to tell you," she said, "before I told them. But they are like a pack of terriers when they get onto something. Shouldn't complain, I suppose. Ought to be grateful to have policemen like that in this day and age. What do you think?"

"Yes, I quite agree. But then what did you wish to tell me first?"

"I think I saw someone going into your house last night. It was a man, and he was either drunk, or he was carrying something awkward..."

What might have been a most interesting narrative was interrupted by Sergeant Holliman who came gliding up behind Mrs. Donahue. "Thank you, Mrs. Donahue," he said. "I've arranged transportation. A policeman is waiting outside. Thank you for your help."

Mrs. Donahue shrugged her shoulders, obediently took her cue and left.

Then Holliman directed his attention toward James and me. To me he was warm and, ironically, paternal. (I was clearly older.) To James he was considerably cooler, curtly ordering him to wait outside while I was being interviewed.

Holliman led me to a chair near an empty desk. It was a desk which, in this environment, was embarrassingly neat.

"I'm very glad you felt up to coming down here today," he said, and then proceeded to shuffle some papers about, arranging most of them in a neat pile at one corner. He placed a pad of lined paper in the center of his desk blotter, removed a silver fountain pen from his inside jacket pocket, uncapped it, made a few notations at the top of the pad, then with pen poised he looked up at me and was about to speak.

"Before we begin," I said, "I would like to point out that I consider James O'Toole a fine policeman..."

"Yes, well..." started Holliman, trying to brush this aside.

"Besides being a close, personal friend," I finished my sentence and continued: "I called him as a friend. Without knowing what was wrong, he came to me as a friend. As soon as he arrived and saw the situation, he called you."

"I believe he was also a close, personal friend of the deceased lady," suggested Holliman.

This took me off guard. I had thought James was in trouble merely for coming alone to the scene of the crime. "I escorted Mrs. Lamphere to a few parties where Mr. O'Toole was in attendance," I admitted. "But I would not call them remarkably close nor personal friends."

"Well, we may have occasion to speak more of your friend later. Let's concentrate now on the business at hand," he diplomatically changed the subject. "I've been told that your health is not of the best at the moment. Do you feel up to discussing what went on last night?"

I nodded. "Please feel free. I am in control."

"Good! Good. Now, if you know—and I don't—what the *beginning* is, I'd appreciate it if you'd start there."

"On last Sunday evening I received a call from Jerome Lamphere in New York. He asked if he might visit over a long weekend. He planned to leave after work on Thursday, arriving Thursday evening."

"And he was coming alone."

"He didn't tell me otherwise, and I doubt he'd surprise me with anyone."

"What time did he plan to leave New York?"

"He said he'd try to leave around 4:15 and thought he could be at my house by 7:30. I told him that Dr. Sterne, Harvard's noted professor of medieval music, and I had a long-standing date for Thursday evenings and that I would not be home until around 11:00. So I gave him instructions on how he could let himself in when he arrived."

"How was that?"

"I keep a key behind a loose tile to the right of the front door."

"Where we found it. Do you think this is fair to your tenants?" he frowned.

"Well," I blushed, "I have only *one* tenant at the moment, an elderly lady who is away for the weekend. We feel quite safe in South Boston. Leaving the key was a convenience for both of us."

He was unimpressed. "Who knew about the key?"

"I made no secret of it among my friends. Jerome knew, of course. And Mrs. Lamphere also had access."

"I suppose your friend O'Toole knew?"

I paused to remember O'Toole arriving at my apartment door the previous evening rather than ringing the bell from outside. "Yes," I said, "I suppose he must have known."

"Even your neighbor Mrs. Donahue may have known of it?"

"Mrs. Donahue?"

"You know her?"

"A fine woman."

"Reliable?"

"Her eyesight is not the best, but she makes every effort to be honest."

"Have you any way of knowing what time Lamphere actually got to your apartment?"

"No."

"Or his wife?"

"No."

"How could we check into these things?"

"Jerome said he was leaving from work. Perhaps his

employer would know the time of his departure."

"How about Mrs. Lamphere?"

"She lives alone in Wessex."

"How would she get here?"

"She drives a green Volkswagen, as I told you."

"Yes, an ignition key was found in her skirt pocket."

"Did you find the car?"

"Did it have any special features, collision damage, any defects?"

"Well, it backfired."

"How long had Lamphere owned his car?"

"It was not his. He borrowed it from a friend, Martha somebody."

"Martha Simms?" asked Holliman.

"Sergeant," I asked with a tone of exasperation, "why are you asking me questions to which you already know the answers?"

He put down his pen, looked at me and smiled. "Just checking, Mr. Webb. That's what police work is, a lot of it, checking the same thing from various angles, like radar."

"I understand."

"You aren't a suspect. We have the testimony of Dr. Sterne and a waitress."

"I'm glad to hear it."

"Miss Simms was contacted in New York City at around 1:30 A.M. How well do you know her?"

"Oh, not very well. I met her only once when I was visiting Jerome in New York. She seemed like a very nice girl."

"Yes, well, let us return to Mr. Lamphere," he resumed, picking up his pen. "Where was he employed?"

"He was a writer for Borman Publications."

"I don't think I know that one," said Holliman as he wrote it "I'm not surprised, Sergeant. They publish what is commonly known as 'fan' magazines."

"And how long had he worked there?"

"Since he left Massachusetts about three years ago. He had been teaching at Briarborough Junior College in Wessex. After ten years of that he left the college to seek his fortune in New York."

"Writing for fan magazines. And I gather he left his wife at the same time."

"Yes."

"You knew the wife well, didn't you?"

"Yes. We had all met in college. I remained a friend to each of them after they separated."

"It isn't easy, is it?" he said, strangely sad. "Did Lamphere mention his wife during your phone conversation?"

"No."

"Did you hear from Mrs. Lamphere during this period?"

"Yes, as a matter of fact, she was with me in my apartment when the call came through from Jerome. I told her of his visit, and we said nothing more about it."

That same inexplicably sad look again crossed his face. I supposed he had lost his own wife one way or another. He looked up and caught my expression, then nodded in answer to the question I never asked. I nodded back.

"Have any strangers approached you at your home in the last few days?" he asked. "Magazine salesmen, someone looking at your vacant apartment, anyone you didn't know personally?"

"No, I don't think so."

"Did either Lamphere or his wife have enemies?"

"None that I know of."

"Any suicidal tendencies?"

"Well..."

"Yes?"

31

"They were both subject to despair, hope and despair, periodically. But I can't believe they'd kill themselves."

"Nor each other?"

"No."

"He sighed. "Have you any idea why either of these people might have died?"

"No, none."

"Are you sure?"

"When Jerome telephoned me he was in a period of hope."

"And Mrs. Lamphere?"

"When I last saw her she was in good spirits."

"Do you know why?"

"I seldom did."

My mind wandered as he made notations on his pad. He looked up after a moment and eyed me curiously. "I was just thinking," I said when I had finally focused on his expression, "about Haydn."

"Who?"

"Joseph Haydn, the composer."

"I'm afraid I don't..." he let the sentence trail off of its own accord.

"Austrian," I explained. "Late Eighteenth Century."

"What's the connection?"

"Well," I said, "a few years ago I received a call from an eclectic friend of mine, an architect who loves but knows very little about music. Someone had offered to sell him an old manuscript reputed to be in Haydn't own hand. So I visited my friend to have a look at what might have been a very important find. But, upon seeing it I was instantly disappointed. It did indeed *look* like Haydn's hand, and nearly everything about it seemed authentic, the paper, the quality of the ink. But I was certain it was *not* in Haydn's hand. I suspected this not on the basis of what I saw, but of what I didn't see. You see, at the beginning of almost every known Haydn manuscript are written the words *In nomine Domini,* in the name of our Lord, and at the end he would write *laus Deo*—praise the Lord, or thank God. Now, my friend's manuscript had neither of these, so it was immediately suspect, again not for what it *had* but for what it did *not* have."

Holliman seemed interested. "That is a principle of police work," he said. "Much can be discovered by what is not there. Such as the green Volkswagen."

"Yes," I said. "And perhaps more than that."

"Was something missing from your apartment?"

"I don't know. There is very little there that anyone would want. I have three or four old music manuscripts, but only one is of any real value."

Holliman put his pen down, placed the pad to one side, reached to the floor on the other side of the desk, brought up a small canvas bag and placed it on the desk where the pen had been. "Do you recognize this?" he asked.

"It was in the room last night. I recognized it as the bag Jerome had brought on his previous visit."

"A previous visit when he used your concealed doorkey."

"Yes."

He unzipped the case and systematically removed its contents. There seemed to be nothing out of the ordinary. Just the kind of things you would expect a fastidious man to bring along on a weekend visit. Four pair of socks, one for each day of his visit, and one to cover the unexpected. The same for underwear, etcetera. A pipe and tobacco... but it would be pointless to complete the list.

"Nothing very interesting to be seen here," suggested Holliman. "Do you agree?" I did. Then I suppose my expression changed as I recalled the dream image of Jerome reading aloud and drinking from a bottle. "Is there something you *don't* see here?" Holliman asked me.

"The last time Jerome visited me he stopped off in the neighborhood for a bottle of Irish whiskey," I said. "It was one of the high points of his visit. Knowing Jerome, it would have been logical for him to follow the same ritual on this visit."

"Anything else missing?"

"Yes, I think so. Something rather obvious, too. You may recall my saying that my friend had reached a period of hope. That was because he was working on a novel, one he was very excited about. He was visiting me to discuss it. So I therefore assumed he'd be bringing some kind of manuscript."

The sergeant was silent for a moment, nodded, picked up his fountain pen, rearranged the pad and began to write. After quite a long time, he made one small precise dot at the end of a sentence, replaced the pen in its top, then looked up at me. "I think, at this point he said, "it might be best for us to visit the scene of the crime. Would you come along?"

"Sergeant, I have to know. Is Officer O'Toole in trouble?"

"That remains to be seen," he hedged.

"In my opinion, he is an admirable policeman."

"He is a good cop," Holliman conceded. "He knows about everything in the book."

"Is there something else?" I asked.

"It wouldn't be ethical to say any more," he shrugged apologetically, "but speaking abstractly, great police work takes many qualities, not the least of which is imagination." He winked at me. "And it is also helpful not to be personally involved with people who get killed." With this, he whisked out, picking up a grim O'Toole on the way. "Come along, O'Toole," he said.

Arriving at my house, we parked in the very spot where

Jerome's car had rested on the previous evening. We got out and approached the house. At Holliman's request, I carefully retraced each step I had taken on the previous evening, from the front door to the bedroom.

The bodies had been removed, but the apartment was a disgrace. A swatch of wallpaper had been removed, my blanket was gone, and there was a dark powder covering nearly everything.

"There are people in business who clean up after us," Holliman consoled me.

"Don't worry," James patted me on the shoulder. "We'll help you, Sarah and me." Then he turned to his superior. "How do we think it happened, Sergeant?"

"Well, it looked like Mr. Lamphere killed Mrs. Lamphere, then committed suicide, doesn't it?"

"I wasn't sure," said James. "But considering the position of Lamphere's hand over the bed and the position of the gun on the floor..."

"Of course," said Holliman, "none of the neighbors *heard* a shot. Not even a car backfiring," he winked at me. "But that may not mean anything."

"True enough," nodded James.

"And of course," continued Holliman, his irony completely lost on my friend, "although Lamphere died of a bullet from the gun, Mrs. Lamphere wasn't shot at all. This fact was missing from your notes, as I recall."

"Well," James slowed, "I was only looking to see if she was alive. But I did overhear you dictating the clubbing idea."

"Would you consider that, if Lamphere intended to kill his wife, he would reserve a bullet only for himself?"

James was silent, and Holliman turned the question to me. "I wouldn't know," I admitted. "I can't believe that Jerome would kill Doris in any case."

"What would you say," asked Holliman, his tone softening to me, "if I told you that Lamphere probably died hours before his wife?"

"But I remember that the blood seemed fresh on both of them."

"Yes," said Holliman, "the blood was moist on both of them. But their body temperatures were decidedly different."

"Then someone killed Jerome by shooting him, waited a few hours and killed Doris with a blow to the head?"

"Looks that way, doesn't it? As it happens, there were fingerprints on the gun. What's more unusual, they seem to belong to three different people: Mr. Lamphere, Mrs. Lamphere and someone else. Often we have trouble finding any fingerprints at all. Here we have found those of three people on one gun. That may mean something, and it may not. Of course, the blood shouldn't be in the condition we found it on Lamphere, still moist and all over his face like that. Nor should those stains," he pointed to the wall where the wallpaper was now missing, "have the configuration they did. What would you say, O'Toole?"

"I agree," he said. "It looks like one of the bodies was wounded, then whirled by the feet to produce those marks, swung in this direction," he motioned north to south. "But if that had happened, there should be other stains in here, and there aren't."

"The stains are green," I offered. "Perhaps it isn't blood."

"That," explained James, "sometimes happens on this colored surface. It's the forming of oxide of copper."

"Just like in the book," Holliman smiled, then turned to James. "Did you ever think to look across the street?"

"Sir?"

"Across the street, Officer O'Toole. Sometimes when

you look across the street you'll see a face flash by a window. That will be the neighborhood busybody, the one who watches the streets and may have seen something. Did you look across the street?"

"I searched this house, sir."

"I'm sure you did, O'Toole," Holliman persisted, "but if you had looked across the street and seen Mrs. Donahue staring back at you, if then you had questioned her, she might have revealed that she saw a man entering this front door. She would have told you he walked strangely as though carrying something, or drunk. She knew Webb was away every Thursday, so she watched until the man came out about fifteen or twenty minutes later. This time, she would have told you, she was certain he was carrying something, perhaps one of those large green plastic garbage bags." He turned abruptly to me. "Do you use them?"

"No," I said. "I disapprove of plastic."

"Anyway," he returned his attention to James, "she would have told you that she watched the building until Webb returned home. No one else entered or left." He paused, letting it all sink in, then turned back to me. "Now, Mr. Webb, would you please put into operation your particular talent for the unseen?"

I opened the small cupboard where I kept my manuscripts. "Well," I said, "this is quite puzzling."

"Yes?" asked Holliman.

"One is missing," I told him. "But the one that's missing is a single page from the Baroque period. It is worth very little. It was colorful, though, and I had intended to frame it to brighten up this room. *This* one," I pulled another[*] from its place, "is worth thousands, and it is untouched."

---

[*] I am not at liberty, at the moment, to describe my valuable manuscript, as I do not wish to sell and do not wish to be plagued by collectors trying to change my mind.

"Well," asked Holliman of James, "where would you suppose the missing manuscript was?"

"In a green plastic garbage bag? With some fence?"

"Good, ordinary guesses," said Holliman. Then he motioned us toward the living room window and raised it. He gestured for me to look outside. I did so, and there was my missing manuscript taped beneath the sill just above the garbage cans.

"That's it," I said.

"Yes," said Holliman. "Leave it there."

"But why?" I asked.

He waved to a man positioned in a window a few houses away. "To see who comes to get it," he told me, "or who doesn't."

Chapter V

Miss Pinkham, contrary to her maidenly character, quietly followed the police reports in the Boston Globe. Now and then, when some especially interesting tidbit came to her attention, she would simply have to share it with someone. It was usually me. I must say I appreciated this little attention, and she did, particularly in the earlier days, come up with items my untrained eye would overlook. But as time went on, and under her tutelage, I became myself something of an authority on recent crime in the area. Therefore, in restrospect, it comes as a shock to me that I never guessed she would know about the incidents in my very home. Holliman was just ushering me out my door when the phone rang, and Miss Pinkham's breathless voice on the other end created a veritable static of question marks.

"Mr. Webb???" After so many years of working together she maintained the formal address. And so it would be forever until one of us was called to that Great Library in the Sky.

"Speaking," I said and waited, for we did not allow ourselves the intimacy of voice recognition.

"This is Miss Pinkham."

"Hello, Miss Pinkham. I trust it was not too difficult for you without me today."

"Not at all. I merely wished to ascertain that you were in good health and that the horrors of the night had not overly upset you."

"I have not read the account, Miss Pinkham, but I am sure they failed to capture the true weight of the incidents which have transpired."

"Oh???" she asked, waiting.

"I will regale you with each detail upon my return."

"Of course you do not wish to speak of it now. Do you anticipate that you will be in on Monday?" And then she added so as not to appear inquisitive, "Someone has been asking about Philibert Jambe de Fer, the *Epitome musical des tons sons accordz*. I thought it would amuse you, and I asked him to come back."

It was a moment of decision. Was I truly prepared to feed the ravenous interest of dear Miss Pinkham? No, my loins were not quite *that* girded.

"As a matter of fact, Miss Pinkham, there is some troublesome police business in which I am required to assist at the moment. In the interest of justice, not to mention a *full* account upon my return, it is best that I take a week of my vacation at the present time. Do you think you can manage without me for that long?"

"Oh yes, of course. Please don't trouble yourself about it. However, should something of an extremely specialized nature come up, may I feel free to call on you?"

"Ah, that may be difficult," I lied. "My business requires me to travel."

"Indeed???"

"To New York City!" I added for emphasis.

"Indeed, that *is* traveling," said Miss Pinkham to whom anywhere outside of Boston was considered a major journey.

And after we had exchanged a few amenities, I replaced the receiver and left the library in extremely capable hands.

Then it occured to me that a trip to New York might not be out of the question.

James and Holliman were waiting for me at the door. "Sergeant," I said, "if I'm not a suspect, there are some details I might be able to help with in New York, things I might do for my departed friend."

"Yes," said Holliman after a moment. "All right, if you keep in touch."

"I will," I assured him. "And do you mind now if I spend the evening in my own house? It would be much more convenient packing-wise."

Holliman considered this and then conceded that, true to the appearance of my apartment, what could be gleaned from it had been, and he gave me permission to stay, after he assured me the building was being watched and that I should be safe. Then he left, James with him, an air of reluctance in their wake.

Once the door had closed between us, I felt that I had placed myself upon a path from which there would be no egress before the end, wherever and whatever that might be.

As Dr. Sterne often said, "There are situations one cannot get around. One has to go through them to get to the other side."

Chapter VI

It had not occured to me to have trepidations about spending the night in my apartment, but others would remind me of my oversight.

"How can you possible spend the night there?" asked Sterne over the telephone, "after all that has passed?"

I had no answer for him. Explaining things to the good doctor had already been difficult. He did not seem alarmed that two close friends had been found dead in my apartment, for these things—by Sterne's Law—merely served to confirm and explain the success of our previous evening. That part was very clear to Sterne. What he found it difficult to comprehend was the possibility of my not being with him the following Thursday. Although he did not say so, he considered this break in ritual a breach of ethics and good manners. On the surface he was most civil and understanding, but beneath this pose I sensed an undoubtable feeling of betrayal.

"Of course, you realize..." he paused trying to hide his disappointment in me. "You realize," he continued, "that the police have asked me to verify your whereabouts of last evening."

"I hope that did not inconvenience you too much," I offered.

He said "No!" too quickly and with apparent effort. "No, it is the least I can do for a friend in need."

"Thank you."

"Think of me Thursday, holding forth at our usual table, a candle lit for your return."

"Thank you," I smiled, appreciating his satire.

"Enjoy New York, and do avoid the Wagner.

Americans simply don't know how to do Wagner, don't you agree?"

As we said goodby I knew he would hang up the receiver hoping that the storm which had disrupted his life would be followed by some inevitable calm. And perhaps, for our affections for each other go deeper than we would bother to acknowledge, perhaps he wished the same for me.

There were several other calls, all expressing sympathy, all offering assistance, all wondering how I could spend the night in my apartment now. But it was James O'Toole, one of the last callers, who went to the heart of the matter.

"Aren't you afraid?" he asked point blank.

I was not. I did not expect the killer to return and I did not believe in ghosts. Ghosts I considered a figment of one's imagination, and I did not consider myself to be any more burdened with that than Holliman thought James was. If I possessed it in quantity I would certainly avoid using it at this time of my life. When I assured James that I was not afraid and that I did not intend to impose on his hospitality a second night, he sounded worried and said he'd be right over.

True to his word, he soon arrived with a bottle of whiskey and a hangdog look. "Ah, my friend, they're being very hard on me... yes, the very department who's got my life blood these many years."

"Why, James?"

"Well, they made some inquiries, and they found out I'd met Dorie. And then it seemed such a strange coincidence, me being at the scene of the crime. Someone told them I'd been seen talking to her at one of our dances... as if there was something wrong with talking... I mean, my wife isn't always easy to talk to..."

I hushed him with a raised hand. We spent the rest of

the night drinking, cursing our fates, and all such customs of which I am in total favor. Late into the evening there was a call from Sarah. O'Toole, filled with hundred proof courage, told her to go to the devil and he'd be home when he was bloody good and ready. He hung up with finality, finished his drink and said he had to be on his way. Wouldn't I reconsider and come with him? I said that I would not and poured him out the door. "You're a brave man, H. Martin Webb," he trailed off toward his vehicle.

I undressed and approached the bed. The image of Jerome clung to it, murdered it is said some hours before his wife whose image still clung to the floor. Some hours before. How long could it be? If he'd left New York at 4:15 and arrived here on schedule, say 7:15? Assume he was shot as he came through the door, or around 7:30, give or take a few minutes. I arrived home at 11:00 or so. He would have been dead no longer than three and a half hours. Well, that was possible, except for the apparent freshness of the blood. In the meantime, I suppose the killer waited here. Why? For me? No. For Doris? Then, with a gun in his hand, why did he club her? She was a strong, robust girl and a blow to the head would be less sure than a bullet. He must have been mad.

"What killer is not?" I asked myself as I brushed Jerome's image from the bed and got into it. I set the clock radio and settled into a fitful slumber.

I dreamt that the Boston Symphony was playing *Bolero*. However, seated next to me was not Dr. Sterne but Doris. She was less corporeal than I and seemed to change shape and color, somewhat erotically. She was crying in harmony with the music.

Then she was in her auto which was moving about the stage and backfiring. As *Bolero* reached its climax, some unseen audience members threw handballs onto the stage. One caught in the tailpipe of Doris' car. The car backfired and the ball shot out.

Then Jerome's image floated before me, the handball in his mouth like a coin placed on the tongue of the dead who were ferried across the River Styx. He drifted away from me into the distance, to a Vivaldi tune, and I heard a bell ringing.

I had no time to consider the meaning of my dream. The phone was ringing as I awoke. Vivaldi was playing on the clock radio. (Among the lesser masters he is the least.)

I sprang from bed and rushed to the phone. I lifted the receiver.

"Hello, Martin Webb? You may not remember me. We met a year ago in New York."

"I remember you," I said. "It is Jerome's friend, Martha Simms, is it not?"

"Yes," she said. "I called to find out about my car. The Boston police tell me they need to keep it. And a Sergeant Holliman mentioned that you're coming to New York."

"Yes," I said. "Today."

"Oh," she paused, "I thought if you came later, you might drive my car back."

"Would you like me to wait?"

"No," she said. "Please don't. It isn't important. I'd much rather see you now. Can we meet?"

"Yes, I'd be happy to."

"Hurry," she said.

Chapter VII

As I looked out my window that Saturday morning, I decided it was going to be another sweltering day. The plain-clothes man in the window beyond my back yard had his shirtsleeves rolled up in anticipation. We waved to each other.

The manuscript was still intact, although the tape seemed to be loosening in the morning's humidity. I pressed it back in place.

Breakfast: three strips of semi-crisp bacon and two eggs up as only I could cook them. (Others had tried and failed miserably.) Also, as was my custom, I enjoyed half a grapefruit, the second half left upside down in a bowl in my refrigerator. How long would I be gone? Would it keep? Never mind, I threw caution to the wind. One could not spend his life worrying about perishables. It was a late breakfast, and leisurely, for I did not expect further sustenance until I rewarded myself for reaching my destination.

It was about 11:00 when I approached the Grey Ghost. There was plenty of time for him to be troublesome, not start, have a flat and so forth, plenty of time for an accident of moderate seriousness, and I still had a reasonable chance of reaching my destination on the appointed day.

Grey Ghost looked friendly. He coughed self-consciously as I turned the ignition, a mere formality which I had come to understand. I paused, held the wheel a moment, then tried again. Another tentative cough, and then the reassuring purr of a superior machine.

We were on our way. Ah, the thrill of that power

around one! Ah, the sublime ecstasy, in a world where the machine is man's acquired, if not actual, enemy... in such a world to see machine and man as one!

We were on our way to adventure. I sensed it but did not consciously understand what it would be. I did not have a clear idea why I was going to New York. Such uncertainties did not concern me. Facing the puzzle of the murders and considering my own health, I knew that each thing must be dealt with at the proper time.

That, in fact, was often the way Jerome dealt with crisis. Once, when the pressure of teaching young, inattentive girls became too much, when his aims exceeded their grasp, when in fact nothing seemed worthwhile or escapable, then he turned only half jokingly to the writings of that grand old Twentieth Century philosopher, Dale Carnegie. He would attempt to live his life in air-tight compartments, not to worry about tomorrow today, as it were. He would try. His final abandonment of all his compartments, including his wife, Doris, was perhaps less of a testimonial than Mr. Carnegie would have wished. But still there was some value in the tired, pragmatic philosophy.

At the moment, I had entered into a compartment of my own. I suppose it was labelled "INVESTIGATION AND ANALYSIS... CAUTION... POTENTIALLY EMOTIONAL MATERIAL." Sub compartment: "Who Died?"

Who were Jerome and Doris to me?

We all attended the same college, but I will not name it because it has since acquired more students, considerably more tuition, more land, more buildings, more debts, and it is a different college.

To pay my then-modest tuition I worked in a record store, the old-fashioned kind with listening booths. On one particular day Doris, whom I already knew from several music classes we shared, brought Jerome in and introduced him to me. He struck me instantly as possessing the contradictory qualities of being likeable and needing to be liked. Doris said she wanted Jerome to hear good old 4433. It was a Columbia release for which the catalog number was ML-4433.

The world's true romantics will know immediately that I refer to the only perfect recording of Rachmaninoff's Second Symphony by the Philadelphia Orchestra under that great master Eugene Ormandy (who, unfortunately, was unable to duplicate the effort in a second recording years later). I pretended to take it from a treasured spot in the racks, cautioned them not to play the third movement without a chaperone, and later as they sat in the booth listening to it, I placed against the window a sign which proclaimed to them, "GOD IS WATCHING YOU!"

Ah, how much happier those days seem now. And yet we were so miserable. Both Jerome and Doris seemed subject to fits of melancholia which they enjoyed to the utmost. I had them also, but since I did not choose to share them I lost the pleasure for which melancholy is intended.

Jerome saw himself in tragic Shakespearean roles. In fact, he studied the Bard quite seriously. But ultimately he could not decide if he was Hamlet or Lear. He quoted both.

Doris pictured herself on the brink of madness. She once confided in me that her great-grandmother suffered from schizophrenia and that she (Doris) did not feel so well herself. It seemed that all she had to look forward to was death by some rare, incurable disease or by being psychologically split asunder.

I suppose it was through the sharing of their sufferings that Jerome and Doris fell in love. Then there was joy, and they enjoyed that even more than the suffering.

Although I pretended to find it intolerable, I was secretly happy for them and became the best man at their wedding, which, as it happened, occurred on the very day Jerome graduated from the unnamed college. "Out of one institution and into another," he was to write me later.

Neither of them ever tested their wings. Jerome stifled Doris' independence, then felt smothered and could not show affection when she became dependent. Needing affection, Doris intensified the problem by making demands. And Jerome escaped the trap he had created, leaving Doris with nothing to lean on. She tottered but through sheer strength avoided falling into the abyss she had collaborated in creating.

I suppose I was there to help save her from the abyss. At the time I was a member of an athletic club, and the man who had for years played piano for the calesthenics class had suddenly passed away, thoughtfully leaving a modest occupation for Doris. It was summer, and the class had shifted to a Monday-to-Thursday schedule. In fact, in honor of summer, the whole building was closed for long weekends. Doris enjoyed the four-day work week, until the financial realities of life crept in on her.

For a while she gained some hedge against creditors by leaving her bill payments in the club late Thursday evenings. Someone would always dutifully find them on Monday morning and mail them. In the meantime, Doris had bought extra time in which to deposit money to cover the checks. And if creditors should take advantage of the weekend to find her at home, she could always tell them, with great sincerity, that the checks were in the mail. This sort of strategy, however, barely outlasted the summer, and then she was forced to seek full-time employment near Wessex, eventually becoming a laboratory technician in her local hospital.

Her new position seemed to contribute to her mental

balance, perhaps because in the midst of death, insanity loses some of its exotic qualities to those who are, in fact, sane.

Although they seldom spoke of their estrangement, nor of their forever-impending divorce, I could only assume that Jerome and Doris remaining legally united was an unspoken agreement between them to retain the symbolic link that bound them together, their need to find sadness in each other.

Who were Jerome and Doris to me? And what drew me to them? It was their strength.

Ah, do not close the book just yet before I explain. I who displayed strength was in fact weak. They who displayed weakness were, in fact, strong. They learned to bend when hit by emotional whirlwinds, and they learned not to break. By nature I am a person who can be adamant about things. But, alas, as the consitution weakened, even I had to learn to lie down, allowing the winds of change to pass overhead.

Yes, their strength. Not just emotional strength. Jerome would hand wrestle with all comers and he would often win against seemingly insurmountable odds. And Doris, though professing weakness, would scoop up a gigantic laundry bag from the ground and heave it into the automobile. I would not care to have tangled with either of them under any circumstances.

Such were my ponderings as I sped at fifty miles-per-hour between Boston and New York, off the Massachusetts Turnpike, onto 84 through Hartford, onto 684, then onto the Sawmill River Parkway. At this point I was reminded of my destination. Heavens! Had it been a full year since I was last in the big city? Yes, over a year.

That time I had found Jerome ensconced in an apartment of moderate size in which he occupied the living room. A room-mate whom I never met and who occupied the only bedroom was, on that weekend, off on some mysterious business. Jerome had mentioned the roommate, suggested something confidential about his occupation, and then the subject was avoided. If the truth were known, I was not very interested, and except for several phone calls for the missing roommate, he was forgotten.

I remembered Martha Simms. She was a most attractive young lady, slender, with long dark hair and a guitar. The guitar was almost obligatory among young ladies of her generation. Out of respect for the Great Masters with whom she assumed I was on intimate terms, she refrained from competing musically.

But when it came to fried chicken, she had no equal, and the three of us—Jerome, Martha and myself—spent a most pleasant evening together.

Much of the time we amused ourselves with literary banter. As Martha carried in a tray of chicken, Jerome misquoted "So foul (fowl) and fair a dame I have not seen," from *Macbeth,* turning a tragic line into a typically horrible Shakespearean pun.

"Now, good digestion wait on appetite/And health on both," I quoted from the same play.

"Pleas't your Highness/To grace us with your royal company?" Jerome asked Martha.

"Got to get the potato salad," she said and returned to the kitchen.

"What ho!" I exclaimed.

"There you go again," said Jerome, "putting a foot in your mouth." He again punned, referring to the metric foot in a Shakespearean line.*

In the pleasure of that evening, a satisfaction and ambience for which the Germans have a totally

---

*i.e. one unaccented and one accented syllable. "What *ho*" would be one of five such feet in a Shakespearean iambic pentameter line.

unspellable word held sway. Everything seemed an excuse for hilarity, and we would laugh uproariously at the drop of a pun. Even Martha, who lacked the background in our long established routine, joined in good naturedly. Thinking back on it, I realize we may have been rude to engage in such flagrant indulgence. Few others shared our passion for words, puns and riddles, but we could have resisted the impulse to indulge no more easily than a desert traveler could avoid an oasis.

Martha did leave us before the evening was over, and I asked Jerome if we had not frightened her away.

"She has a date with Al Lees," he said, lighting his pipe. I was silent until he laughed. "Come, come, where is thy wit? *Al Lees*!"

"Oh," I said. "Al Lees. Alias. It's not very funny."

"No," he said, suddenly serious, then thoughtfully blowing smoke into the air, "I guess it isn't."

It was not until later that evening as we were walking to the local Y.M.C.A. where Jerome was a member and where I insisted on staying, that he mentioned he was planning a book. But he was reluctant to talk about it, he said, because talking was the opposite of writing, and one often precluded the other.

Shortly after my visit, I had received a letter from him, one filled with optimism. "Al Lees has been dispatched," he wrote. "Martha now shares my living room. And the novel is begun!" In letters to follow, he never failed to mention the novel. "I am at least consistent," he wrote. "A page a day whether I need it or not."

Recently he had written that the novel was near completion and that Martha had found a place of her own.

I was distracted from my ruminations by the New York skyline. Its vitality shone, to my mind, with some great eternal energy. I felt it draw me as I entered onto the West

Side Highway, a road which skirts the edge of the city as though afraid to enter, but hospitably offering a variety of exits to the adventurous or foolhardy. As I have already written, I was on an adventure. For the moment, I did not consider the foolhardy part.

Chapter VIII

The highway was heavily occupied by too many cars moving much too fast for their proximity to each other. It was with much difficulty and great relief that I managed to wend my way into the right lane in time for my exit.

Continuing the pattern, there were, of course, too many cars and no parking places on West 84th Street, except near an open hydrant, and that was taken up by children avoiding the heat of the day. I was forced to double park and, with one eye ever on the Grey Ghost, I dashed through a front door and rang the bell by Martha's name.

"Come up," she invited through the intercom. After I'd explained the situation, she said that she'd come down, which she did with admirable promptness.

She placed a garbage bag atop a can and embraced me. "I'm so glad you're here," she said into my shoulder. She looked up at me, then self-consciously stepped back, returned to the garbage can and deposited the bag she had left on its lid. She looked more than a year older. Now her hair was worn up in a bun seeming to accentuate an unnatural severity in her features. There were circles under her eyes, and her strong jaws were tightly set. The weeping was past.

"Was Jerry murdered?" she asked, replacing the lid and turning to me.

"Apparently. Although there was some amateurish attempt to make it look like suicide."

"How do you mean?"

"Which? That it was made to look like suicide, or that it was an amateurish attempt?"

"Well . . . both."

"The bodies were in such a position to suggest that Jerome had killed Doris by hitting her over the head before shooting himself."

"Yes?"

"However, Jerome died first, perhaps several hours before. Therefore, unless we are to assume that Doris shot Jerome and waited around several hours before fatally striking herself over the head, we must assume that there was a third party. And an amateur," I continued, picking up an earlier thread, "especially when you consider one of my musical manuscripts was purloined . . . however, the *least* valuable of those I presently own."

She looked away, distracted by the noise of the children. "That could mean that the murderer wanted to make robbery appear to be the motive, but didn't want to hurt you more than necessary."

"A strange afterthought, considering he had just murdered two of my closest friends. At any rate, the manuscript was found taped outside a window."

"Why?"

"It's something burglars do," I told her, reflecting on one of my past conversations with the knowledgeable Miss Pinkham. "They sometimes hide the evidence near the scene of the crime rather than risk being caught with it. Then later, when attention is off the premises, they return."

"I see," she said, turning back to me. "I'm glad you're here. It's a comfort. Was it hard getting away from Boston?"

"No, not very. I'm not a suspect, myself. So I thought I'd come here and see if there wasn't something I could do, take care of Jerome's things, something."

"He has some things here," she pointed up toward the fourth floor of the building, a small gabled window. "He always had a complete change of clothes and so forth."

"One to wear and one to wash," I smiled.

"You knew Jerry," she said.

"Would there be a manuscript?" I asked.

"The novel? No, he took that with him. Is it lost?" I nodded. "I don't know anything about it," she said. "Jerry never wanted to discuss it with anyone. In my case, I think he was afraid I'd say something negative. I probably would have."

"You would?"

"He was always trying to work out things on paper that he should've been trying to work out in reality . . . like the thing with Dorie. Every now and then he'd ask her how the divorce was coming along. Each time she'd tell him she was seeing the lawyer next week. It was always next week. We've lived three years of next weeks."

"Were you hoping to marry?"

"Hope gets lost in 'next weeks'!"

"Yes, that must be difficult."

"I couldn't even get it off my chest because he didn't want to discuss it with me. He said that when he got divorced he didn't want me to feel connected with it in any way. He said that would place an unnecessary burden on our relationship. Like having a three-year affair with a married man didn't place any burdens on our relationship! Oh . . . I suppose I'm well out of it. At least I'm still young."

"Don't you think he was also frustrated by the situation?"

"Not the way I was. I actually tried to slug him a couple of times. But he was too strong for me. I don't think I'm any stronger than you are. Excuse me."

"That's all right. I think you probably are stronger than I."

"I'm not stronger than anybody," she said. "I'm glad you're here," she repeated again. "I wish you could stay with me, but it's just a small studio apartment."

"I shall be quite comfortable at the Y where I stayed last time."

"Ridiculous! That would be silly! With all the friends I have in town? I won't hear of it."

She wouldn't, either. The corollary to Sterne's Law would probably be stated: WELL-MEANING FRIENDS WILL STRIVE TO MAKE YOU UNCOMFORTABLE. How often friends had insisted that I have another bite to eat, that I meet their unmarried friends, that I accompany them to a bad film because it might be fun, that I let them drive while I "relax," or—perhaps worst of all—that they be permitted to wash my dishes. Despite my references to my failing health, some will understand that to have lived to my age (which I am not going to reveal) and to have done so as a bachelor has required a generous outlay in intestinal fortitude.

Unprotesting, I allowed Martha to sit behind the wheel of the Grey Ghost and drive me downtown, ending up on a rather pleasant street in that part of New York the inhabitants call Chelsea.

"No parking place," she said. "You might know."

"There's one," I said, for as usual I was watching the *other* side of the street. But it being a one-way street (Sterne's Law had not developed a corollary for that) the spot was too small. Undaunted, she double-parked. I sighed and asked, "Where are we?"

"Don't you remember?" she asked. "This is where you visited Jerry. This is where he lived with his roommate. Didn't you ever meet him?" She put my car keys in her shirt pocket.

"No," I said. "The time I was here, you remember, the

roommate was away."

"Oh yes, that's right. Come along then. It's time you met Harold."

My heart sank. I have never liked the name Harold.

Chapter IX

Martha had a set of keys, and she let us into the building and the apartment. She whistled the first four notes of Beethoven's *Fifth* as we entered. The notes were returned like an echo from the room at the other end of the moderately long hallway, where a man was seated at a table and talking on the telephone, his back toward us. His hand raised briefly in greeting.

The apartment was much as I remembered it. Three doorways opened off the right of the hallway, and were, in fact, open. I saw briefly a cluttered bedroom on my right by the entrance. As we proceeded down the hallway, there was the bathroom, and then a closet-sized kitchen with exposed bricks on one wall. At the end of the hallway was the living room, distinguished only by a pseudo-brick fireplace structure which was used to hold books, and at the front of the building, two windows which came almost to the floor.

As we entered, the man who was obviously Harold swiveled his chair around to greet our approach, waved at us to gesture us in, then swiveled back to his conversation. Martha and I sat down on a wide sofa facing the windows and we waited.

Harold was a youth in his early twenties. He had dark, curly hair and wore large round glass frames without any lenses. The table in front of him was littered with papers, books and what appeared to be manuscripts in cardboard binders.

"Okay, well look, I have to hang up now," he was saying into the receiver. "Some people just came in. Yeah. Well, just do like I said. Call Georgie and *ask* him if he'd be willing to do sound *and* play the part. Sure, he will. He's been nude before. He just won't go for any front shots. Self-conscious, I guess. I don't know. What? (riotous laughter) Well, it's the only part of him that *isn't* up tight. (More laughter) Okay, well look, I've got to go. What?"

The conversation proceeded along this route, getting increasingly graphic for another five minutes before Martha thought of something to say.

"You can see nothing much has changed," she pointed to an ancient radio on the bookcase behind us, then patted the dilapidated sofa we were sitting on. "Still this stuff they found on the street." She pointed to a desk near one of the windows. "That's where he worked. They found the desk on the street, too. Can you imagine someone throwing that away? I wonder if...?" She got up abruptly and began searching through the drawers.

"Okay, look, I've really got to go," said Harold into the telephone. "Michael, can't I call you back? You're not at the studio? Where? Just a minute." He grabbed a piece of paper from the table in front of him, examined it carelessly, turned it over and wrote something. "Okay. Got it. What? I don't know what I'm going to do. You know anybody? Their half would be $117 and change. But the electricity can be murder. Well, look, I don't want to talk about it. Not now. I'll call you. Okay? Okay. Take care." He replaced the receiver, then got up and approached me with his hand outstretched. "Hi. I don't think we've met. I'm Harold. You must be Marty."

"How do you do." I shook his hand. "I've heard Jerome talk about you.

"Don't believe a word of it," he smiled wryly. Then to Martha: "You're wasting your time. The fuzz has already been through that stuff." Then back to me: "It's a terrible thing, isn't it? How could such a thing happen? We take our lives in our hands every day we go out on the streets in this city. And Jerry goes to Boston and gets it there. I couldn't believe it when Martha called to tell me about it."

"I hope I didn't wake you," she said.

"Are you kidding? What was it, 1:30? Georgie was here. I was having a few drinks. 1:30, right?"

"Oh, much later than that."

"Whatever."

"I've come to New York," I said, "to see if there was anything I could do, about arrangements, his things."

"Sure," said Harold. "Let's see. Come on." I followed him obediently to the bathroom where he opened the medicine cabinet and pointed to some toiletries. "These are his," he lowered his voice as though to exclude Martha from hearing. "Not much. He took most of his bathroom stuff with him." He moved to the open bathroom window and shuffled through some bottles on the sill. "None of this is his." Then he pointed across a diamond-shaped air shaft to the kitchen window. "I see something there." He began to reach for it, then decided it would be easier just to go into the kitchen.

Once there, he pointed out two identical bottles of bourbon on the sill, one marked "Jerry," the other marked "Harold."

"This is how we kept from fighting," he continued with his quiet, confidential tone. "We had 'his' and 'his' everything. Of course when one of us ran out, 'his' might become mine. But he's still got half a bottle here. You might as well take it before I do."

"I can't believe it," said Martha hovering in the doorway.

"Don't get snide," he told her, then to me: "She thinks I'm an alcoholic." Then back to her: "I don't have to have one as soon as I get up, do I? I wait 'til five o'clock, don't I?"

"But you'd never make it *past* five," she grinned.

He pushed past her into the living room. "Most of what he owned is in this room, except for that stuff on the table. That's mine. So help yourself. But I really don't think anything here is really worth anything, though. It's up to you. I've been on the phone with his parents upstate. They're not concerned about his stuff. They're pretty broken up. I was, too. But we've got to keep going, don't we? Got to pay the rent."

"I understand what you mean," I said significantly.

"And his wife, too. It's terrible. Do they know who did it yet?"

"No, not yet." Here I reviewed some of the details which I will not again impose on the reader.

"Yeah, the novel," Harold said following my monologue. "I kept telling him there was no money in it. I wanted him to write me a screenplay. See these?" He lifted a pile of manuscripts from the table, then let them fall. "Junk! I wanted Jerry to write me something good. I had this great idea for a story about a folk singer who comes to New York from Tennessee, and about her experience with the agent, and getting sold into white slavery. It'd be a triple-X, but it could really say something, you know? I was gonna talk Martha into writing the music.

"About the novel," I interrupted him. "Was there a copy?"

"I guess he took the only one with him," said Harold. "Can't imagine what happened to it. Where are you staying?"

"He says the Y," said Martha.

"What for? Stay here. We can talk about things. Maybe we can figure things out. That thing pulls out into a bed."

"Can you imagine why anyone would want to take it?" I persisted, oblivious to the lack of transitions in the conversation.

"Sure I can," said Harold in direct response to my question. "But he asked me not to talk about it."

There was a heavy pause. Martha perked up noticably and poised waiting for me to say something. In the pause I took care to choose my words.

"Now that Jerome has passed on," I began, "there may be little point in your otherwise commendable restraint. Whatever you know about the manuscript might help uncover the murderer."

"What murderer?"

"Well, the one..."

"For God's sake, Harold," Martha interrupted, "are you consciously trying to be difficult?!"

"Look, Martha, don't start on me, okay?"

"Well, here we all sit with Jerry dead, and you know something. I mean, obviously. And shutting up about it isn't going to do any good for anybody. So why don't you just say it and stop waiting for people to coax it out of you? We don't especially need your little dramas right now."

"Martha, I know you're upset about Jerry, but lay off me, okay? Stop testing me, okay? It just might be that you wouldn't want me to say what I've got to say. Okay?"

"Well, did you read it?"

"No, I didn't read it." His hurt voice now took on an edge.

"Then what do you know?"

"Nothing. I don't know anything. Okay? You satisfied?"

Martha said something profane, snatched up her purse and made her exit down the hallway, apparently into the bathroom, slamming the door behind her.

When she was gone, Harold let out a long-suffering sigh. "She always assumes the worst of me," he said. "She really knows how to turn me off. I guess it's because my being here always made her feel more like a guest than the lady of the house. Look, come back later tonight without her. Then we can talk."

In the bathroom, Martha coughed.

"She always assumes the worst," he continued and was interrupted by the phone ringing. "Hello? Oh, hi there, where you been? What's up, tiger? Sounds serious. Well, look..." (We heard water running) "Hold on a minute, okay? Just hold on." He cupped his hand over the receiver, and he spoke directly to me. "You see, the novel, it was a murder mystery. And Jerry was using people he knew, me, you, Martha, lots of people."

"Himself?"

"Sort of. He's the one who gets killed in it. He had this feeling that anyone would have a motive for killing anybody. So he started to think about the people around him and why each of them might want to kill him, and that's what got him started." In his excitement he had forgotten to shield his caller from these revelations, and he was gesturing with his hand. "He really got into the whole idea of him being murdered and the killer getting away with it. He did a lot of research, a lot of studying and planning."

"Did he tell you which one of us was supposed to have killed him?"

"Well, no, but I can guess..." (We heard the tap turned off and a toilet flush.) "Look, come back later without her, okay? I don't want to talk in front of her because she wouldn't understand, I mean about Jerry imagining his own death. I think it'd upset her. Besides..." The bathroom door opened suddenly, and he went back to the phone. "Look. Georgie, you're the best sound man in the business as far as I'm concerned. But until Michael knows it, take off your pants. What's the difference? Look, why don't I talk to him? He doesn't need a front shot there. Or you could wear your disguise."

Martha walked into the room, surveyed the scene and said cooly, "Are you sufficiently instructed in telephone technique? If so, why don't we go? Or I'll wait for you in the car?"

I was somewhat torn. Even though I didn't particularly like Harold any more than I have ever liked any Harold (or Hal), his bearing up under Martha's onslaught, in an attempt to spare her feelings, was somewhat commendable. However, it did seem to me that he might have handled it in a more diplomatic way.

"I have to go," I said to Harold, and I got up.

"Hold it a minute, Georgie. Just a minute!" Then to me: "See you later tonight then."

"No, I think not."

"Sure. Come back. Spend the night. We'll have a few drinks, *talk about things*! Who knows what'll float to the top? How long you in town for?"

"I'm not sure."

"You coming, Martin?" Martha started for the door.

"Yes," I said. "I have to go."

"Wait, I'll walk down with you." As we were going out the apartment door, I heard him saying, "Georgie, I've got to see some people off. I'll call you right back. You at home? Okay." He caught up with us on the stairs. "When you going back to Boston?" he asked me. "You know, I've got to go there tomorrow night for a day or two. Maybe I could stay at your place."

I couldn't understand his behavior. Despite a redeeming grace, he seemed oblivious to the tense situation he had precipitated, however good his intentions. He simply would not let us go! As we got to the car, Martha unlocked the driver's side, got in and unbolted the door on the passenger side. Harold was there ahead of me, opening the door, I thought for me. But as I made to get inside, he reached into the back and removed my suitcase.

"This yours?" he decided. "I'll take it up for you."

"No, really," I protested, "I'd much rather stay at the Y."

"____it, Harold," Martha ordered, "put that back!"

"Naw, you don't want to spend your money on the Y. How much do you make a week? Come on back. Stay as long as you want. I'll give you a key. Be good to have someone here while I'm gone. At least you can spend the night. You know, just the two of us. We'll drink, and we'll talk about *things*, okay?"

I thought I detected a note of pleading in his voice, a particular quality that had no doubt been successful with young ladies. It seemed to move even me. Something about him, for a moment, seemed to belie everything else about him, his rudeness, his brashness, his name. There was something else. I was intrigued in spite of myself.

"It's very kind of you," I said. "Very well, then. Perhaps one night."

"Terrific!" said Harold and dashed off with my luggage before I could change my mind. "I'll be waiting for you," he called over his shoulder. "Anytime. I'm up to all hours. You like steak?" And he disappeared into the building.

Chapter X

We took off like a shot, Martha steaming at what she must have considered my lack of character. Feeling much like a small boy who had been naughty, I sat quietly awaiting my punishment.

"You shouldn't let him get his way like that," she said as she finally slowed the car. "He's bad enough. He doesn't need encouraging."

"It must have been very difficult for you seeing Jerome in that setting." A long pause. "Three is a crowd." I bit my tongue.

"With him, two is a crowd," she said and began to laugh ever so slightly. "Jerry was looking for a place of his own, you know. He said that others sapped his creative energies. But what was happening was Harold was imposing on Jerry's territory. Harold would take phone calls in the living room, which also happened to be Jerry's bedroom and study. And Harold might grab a page from Jerry's latest manuscript to make notes, write down phone numbers and so forth. He'd just take things. I don't know if he was a kleptomaniac or just thoughtless." She glanced at me and smiled. "I don't know. You might be able to get something out of him tonight. And then he'll be out of town for a couple of days. It may be okay. Anyway, now I want you to meet some other people you could stay with, in case it doesn't work out with Harold."

We pulled onto a street some ten blocks from Harold's, a quiet, tree-lined street bordered by townhouses. Martha pulled up beside one, and we got out. "This is where Jerry lived when he first came to New York," she said.

We moved up the steps and rang the bell. Moments

later, the door was opened by a silent, smiling giant. He wore a plain white tee shirt and a striped bow tie around his bare neck.

"Boris," Martha greeted him, "this is H. Martin Webb, a good friend of Jerry's."

Boris squeezed my arm. "Bless you," he said. "Beautiful."

I was about to ask him what was beautiful when two children came screaming down the stairs. They stopped, looked hostilely at me and then went screaming back, their piercing sounds disappearing into the upper recesses of the house, faintly heard like the first dull pains of an impacted tooth. Since they contribute nothing to this narrative, I see no point in describing them further. In fact, I shall henceforth ignore their existence. They are not old enough to be in this kind of story, anyway.

Boris leaned down and placed his arm around my shoulder, then guided me to the living room which had one red brick wall, and everything else was painted white. It was a large room, refreshingly open and uncluttered. Some cushions were scattered about the floor. A small, purple divan seemed embarrassed against the wall. Seated on it was a short, compact woman whose rough denim clothing seemed to contradict a soft, Renaissance figure. She sat quite alert, it seemed, her antennae moving about to pick up and react to every conceivable human vibration. After a moment of wide-eyed contemplation, she nodded to Boris.

"H. Martin Webb," Boris told her, and then he explained to me, "This is Empie. I'm her husband."

Empie held out her hand, and I took it awkwardly. "*H. Martin Webb,*" she murmured.

"You want to know what the 'H' stands for," I dared to venture.

"If you wanted people to know that, you wouldn't use an initial."

"Yes," I admitted, somewhat charmed by her sensitivity.

"Martha," she said, and they hugged each other. "Are you all right?"

"Yes, I'm fine now."

"Boris and I would like to do a piece for Jerry," Empie told her, then turned to include me. She must have caught me in a confused expression, for she then explained, "An art piece, something to commemorate his life."

"They do lovely things," Martha told me. "I've been a part of some of them. Jerry, was, too, once." She turned back to Empie. "Tell him."

"No," said Empie. "Boris likes to tell it."

Boris smiled broadly at the opportunity. "You know Picasso's 'Guernica'?" he asked. I nodded, as I remembered the famous mural which froze forever the horror of the 1937 air strike of a peaceful town in Picasso's native Spain.

"And you remember My Lai?" Again I nodded. Could anyone forget the late *Life* magazine's photo of people massacred in a Vietnam village?

"Shortly after My Lai," he continued, "some of us went to the Museum of Modern Art and held a service in front of 'Guernica.' I gave a sermon. Our kids placed flowers in front of it. We had a hassle with the guards about bringing flowers in. They finally allowed the flowers, but Martha had to leave her guitar in the checkroom. If they knew we had it, they probably wouldn't have allowed the blood either."

"Blood?" I asked.

"We got it from the butcher and smuggled it in in the plastic bags. During the ceremony we sprinkled it on the flowers. Beautiful."

"And you call this an art piece?" I asked, just for clarification.

"Art," explained Empie, "is no longer only two-dimensional, framed, painted canvas. This is art," and she pointed over the fireplace to a framed canvas of sky and clouds, "but so is this," and she pointed to a corner of the room where was displayed a replica of a back stoop, railing, clothesline and laundry... all painted blue with clouds. "These were made by Boris. And these," she said "are mine."

She referred to some parchment-like tapestries with poems, or words, such as:

> *death*
> *ISN'T SO BAD*
> *WHEN YOU THINK ABOUT*
> *it.*

and another:

> *Never give a maker*
> *an even buck.*

and there was also a black box which flashed the word "OUCH!" off and on.

"Art is experience," she said. "And life offers a wealth of experiences to those of us who haven't tied ourselves down with rules, laws and taboos. All of life ought to be art. Everything is art. Even you."

"Thank you," I said.

"Heating saki would be nice," said Boris. Empie nodded, and he went into the adjoining kitchen, happily occupying himself with things I could not see.

"Death is art, too," said Empie.

"Some of the best art is death," Boris called from the kitchen.

"He likes funerals," Empie explained. "Was Jerry's death a natural one?" I reacted, and she answered my reaction. "I use the word 'natural' as I think you'd use it, meaning heart attack and so forth."

"I guess I wasn't very explicit," said Martha.

"It was after one o'clock," Empie patted her shoulder. "You aren't used to late hours."

"I don't know what I told you," Martha said. "I just know it was very, very late." She looked pleadingly to me, and I explained the circumstances surrounding Doris and Jerome's deaths.

"I'm not surprised," said Empie when I had finished, and again I reacted. "I mean," she smiled, "I've never know anything productive to come of procrastination. Quite the opposite. Look at her." She pointed to Martha who had been slumped over but sat up when she became the focus of attention. "When I first met her, she had her head together and was in love with Jerry. But she thought she had a covenant, that Jerry would get divorced within a reasonable space of time and would share his freedom with her. Now look at her, unsure of herself as she never was before. That's Jerry's work... or rather his lack of work, his procrastination. He let his love wither on the vine."

"It wasn't all his fault," Martha protested quietly.

"Bull!" said Empie. "What's that expression your father used?" she asked Boris.

"Hmm?" asked Boris, returning with a tray.

"About fishing," she said impatiently.

"Fish or cut bait?" he asked, offering us each a small toy cup, then pouring warm, colorless liquid from what resembled a small bud vase.

"Fish or cut bait, right." Empie leaned toward me. "You knew both of them, Jerry *and* his wife, right?" I nodded. "They must have been two of a kind, two passives, right?"

"Well," I said, "I'm not sure."

"Dorie was," said Martha, sipping her saki. "At least she was as Jerry imagined her. He had this image of her snowed into that cottage in Wessex with the furnace busted down, and she was freezing, with her only hope being some horny derelict on snowshoes being able to find his way up the snowbound driveway. It sounded very passive to me."

"Right," said Empie, "and two passives do *not* make a positive. I'll tell you about passives. They sit around waiting for people to make their decisions for them, and when nobody does, they get angry. They boil inside, until it finally comes out as violence. That's why I wouldn't have any trouble believing that Jerry somehow was responsible for the carnage."

"He was a good man," offered Boris. "He really was, I thought."

"So are you, honey," said Empie going to the kitchen, "but that doesn't change anything. Remember when he came here to stay? He'd just left his wife. He got sick a lot, vomited once a day practically. I made a special tea for him that helped his stomach. But we couldn't help his basic weakness."

"Uh huh, I see," said Boris.

"Maybe we made him leave too soon," Empie wondered. "I thought he was ready to stand alone, but maybe I was wrong."

"You made him leave?" I asked, coughing from my first taste of saki.

"Yes, I told him it was time he controlled his own life, that he'd reached the point of diminishing return in our house, and it was time he left."

"And he did."

"Yes. And he promised not to come back. But what's the difference? He could still find people to lean on. Martha knew how to make the tea for him. He just gravitated to his kind, to Harold." She returned from the kitchen with more saki which she poured into our cups.

"Did you ever see one of his movies?"

"Whose?"

"Harold's. Didn't you know?"

"Know what?"

"Harold," Martha told me, "is a famous pornographic film star called Peter Piper."

My mind flashed back to my drive through Boston's combat zone on Thursday. "IN PERSON - SUNDAY AND MONDAY ONLY - PETER PIPER." So that was why he had to go to Boston the next day. "No," I confessed, "I didn't know."

"Know why he's so popular?" asked Empie. "It's because he always takes the passive role; it's always done *to* him without much effort on his part. He's the perfect tool. Now, we need passives, right, Boris?"

"Uh huh," said Boris agreeably.

"But the actives have to keep them separated or there's going to be chaos. If we see them getting together we have to separate them by any means available. I don't exactly believe in murder, but if that's what it takes, then do it in the best possible way."

"Beautiful," said Boris.

"What way is that?" I asked.

"Well, you could get a cop to do it," she answered. "A cop would know how to do it without getting caught or getting you involved. If I wanted to kill somebody I'd get a cop to do it." When she saw there was no response to that, she continued, "Cops are misinterpreted. They're best for *doing* murders, not for solving them."

"Then who's to solve them?" I asked.

"Why do they have to be solved?"

"Well," I stumbled, "we can't have people going around killing other people, can we?"

"You see?" she smiled. "That's the trouble with people who think too much. Life is action, experience, like I said.

That's why passive people are out of it." She studied my face for a moment, expectantly, then added, "Look, what I think I'm saying is two people died who probably didn't know how to live anyway. Let the rest of us get on with life! Let's do something positive. Let's do some kind of memorial to Jerry and Doris. Let's have a party and exorcise their spirits from life, positively and with love. She snapped her fingers, intrigued with her own idea. "When did they die? Thursday? Okay, this Thursday we'll have a party here, a memorial service of life. What do you think, Boris?"

"Beautiful," said Boris.

"Martha, are you still coming here after work Monday?"

"Yes."

"Good. Bring Martin. We'll work out the details together. It can be a wonderful memorial. And everyone's welcome, everyone who ever knew either of them. You guys invite anybody you want to, okay? We're going to have the best——funeral Chelsea ever saw."

"That's really beautiful," said Boris.

Chapter XI

There being no reasonable means for one of modest means to park a car in New York, Martha offered to look after the Grey Ghost during my stay. She assured me that would be wisest since I was not trained, as she was, to move a car to alternate sides of the street. Just one contravention, she assured me, might be very costly, not to mention infuriating. There would be an excessive fine *and* a towing charge. And since the Boston police were so thoughtfully looking after her own auto, she felt inclined to care for mine. I was reluctant at first, but finally succumbed to her arguments. I only hoped the Grey Ghost (a one-man car) would not hold it against me in future.

"Perhaps tomorrow night you will be my guest at the opera or some such frivolity," I suggested as a repayment for her kindness.

"Yes," she said, "I'd like that. And Monday you'll come to the office and talk to Mr. Bob."

"Who?"

"The man Jerry worked for, my boss." We were now ensconced in the Grey Ghost and she proceeded to drive me the few blocks to Harold's apartment.

Yes, this "Mr. Bob" might be helpful, as perhaps Empie and Boris had been in filling in the puzzle, a puzzle not of who killed whom, but of who was killed. It was now clear that Jerome was not the same person to others as he was to me. And people saw different things in Doris. Since they could no longer speak for themselves, all that could be known of them, all they were now, was a composite of the pieces of themselves they had left with others.

Putting the pieces together was interesting, but with it came the necessity of dealing with strangers. Empie and Boris alone should have filled my yearly quota, but alas, there were probably many more to come.

Since a parking spot conveniently awaited us, I could only assume Martha had no intention of parking. "I won't go up with you," she said, seeing that the light was on in the living room. "I feel funny about the way I acted before. Now look, he may not be home in spite of what he said, or he may be on the phone. If he is home he'll be on the phone. So take the keys. This one's for downstairs and this one's for upstairs. Okay? Goodnight." She impulsively leaned over and gave me a kiss on the cheek. "I'm glad to find out you're the nice man I thought you were."

I could only manage a foolish grin as I alighted and the car went screeching off. Alas, Grey Ghost!

There was, as she had led me to expect, no response to the bell. I let myself in downstairs and walked up to the apartment. As I opened the door I called "hello." Even though the lights were on and music playing, there was no answer. Well, I thought, he has probably stepped out for a minute, to a corner store, or the incinerator, or wherever people go briefly.

The door to Harold's bedroom was open. My attention was drawn to a poster on the wall. "*Hot Peppers*—Introducing Peter Piper," it proclaimed, and this was the only copy to supplement a few suggestive line drawings. It was an effective poster in that it attracted me into a room where I had no business being. There were other posters. "*Southern Comfort*—with Peter Piper, star of *Hot Peppers*." And "Peter Piper in *Bad Guy*." In spaces left over and too small for Peter Piper posters there were various antiques and junque, including a couple of rusty civil war pistols, perhaps props from *Southern Comfort*. I tore myself away and proceeded to the living room.

Once there, I sat on the sofa to await Harold's return. Judy Collins was singing from the radio just behind the sofa. The Whale Song. Although Miss Collins is no Lena Horne, the melody was pleasant enough, and the whales were exceptionally talented at rendering mournful cries. The cries faded out, almost lulling me into a saki-flavored sleep. Then some offensive modern "music" played, and I kneeled on the sofa to reach behind and turn off the radio. It was then that I saw Harold lying behind the sofa, his glassy eyes staring through his glassless frames, turned upward in my direction. Some long-dried spittle on his cheek seemed to point to a gaping mouth which held a dead and silent scream.

Chapter XII

So much for Harold. And so much for all I had hoped to learn from him.

This unfortunate event caused me great personal inconvenience. It is awkward, at the very least, to have the misfortune, ill timing and bad taste to discover more than one corpse within a three-day period.

The police came. I was questioned. The somewhat famous body was treated in the manner to which it had been accustomed, i.e. carefully examined and photographed. Then it was carted off without ceremony.

An autopsy seemed to prove to everyone's satisfaction that (1) Harold had died while I was with Martha, Empie and Boris, and (2) Harold had died from poison* in Jerome's leftover bourbon. Apparently, Harold had finished his own bottle which was empty and had started on his inheritance which was now three-quarters empty on the kitchen windowsill. I recalled it had been half empty earlier in the day. I found myself in the rather bizarre situation of having police in two cities concerned about my whereabouts. The New York contingent, however, proved very helpful and offered to keep Boston informed while I was in their city. They even guaranteed me reservations at the local Y. Boston, in turn, offered to keep New York informed when, and if, I returned. At least I was not going to have to worry about certain details.

Nor, in fact, should you. Suffice it to say, I was kept at the police station that night. Although I was not under arrest, it was suggested that it might be helpful were I

---

*No useful purpose could be served by revealing the name of the potion that done him in.

around. I wished to cooperate, so that night and most of the next day I lived on strong coffee, tasteless sandwiches, cat naps and questioning. How long had I known the deceased? Who were his friends? What brought me to New York? I was not very helpful.

Martha met me at the station late on Sunday. After she had herself been questioned, she sat down on the bench beside me. "They say we can go," she said. "You look pale. Are you feeling all right?"

"The vestiges of an old complaint," I told her, "one that I am managing to keep under control. However, the excitement of the past few days now makes a simple monk's cell at the Y seem very, very attractive." In deference to my condition, she did not protest.

It was about 6:30 in the evening as we emerged from the station. The heat of the day was now settling back into the pavement, watered here and there by open hydrants, further assisted by splashing, half-naked children.

As I alighted from the Grey Ghost at the local Y.M.C.A., Martha offered to pick me up the next morning. Wishing to place no restrictions on my morning, I told her to give me the address and I would meet her at her office. She offered not to go to work, but I thought it wise that we both keep ourselves occupied. She handed me a business card, and I waved goodbye.

It was with great relief that I finally climbed the mountainous steps to the front entrance of the Y. Opening the first set of doors, I was confronted with another flight leading to more doors which opened to the lobby. I looked up as if beseeching strength, then noticed a motto in large letters stretched above the entrance:

ENTER HERE TO BE AND FIND A FRIEND.

"Heaven forfend!" I thought, "let it be Morpheus." I envisioned a solitary room, some few moments of private reflection and rest.

Of course, this was not to be.

Chapter XIII

"*Martin*, my boy!" a voice hit me from behind as I entered the lobby. I turned to see James O'Toole barreling toward me with his arms outstretched. He was wearing civilian clothes, and I wondered if his being implicated in the messy affair had caused him to be drummed out of Boston's finest.

"James," I said, "what are you doing here?"

"Well now, we couldn't have you subjected to the evils of this city without some protection, now could we?" He was playing his Irish cop to the hilt. "Ah, but if the truth were known, there just aren't any worthy handball players left in Boston. No real drinkers, either. Which is it to be?"

"Well, I'm not sure," I said. "First, I really ought to register."

He nodded, accompanied me to the desk and introduced me to the desk clerk, a Mr. O'Brien, who had apparently become James' close, personal friend within the last hour or so.

"Is the gym open?" I asked him, fearing that it might be.

"Not on Sundays," said O'Brien.

"Except to visitors," said James.

"Except to visitors named O'Toole," said O'Brien.

Apparently, O'Brien was distressed that today's Young Men's Christian Association had members that were neither men nor Christians. Also, he was sympathic to the Irish causes championed by James, who was both a man and a Christian. It was therefore a small matter to bend the rules and open the handball courts to us. We were given keys and confidential instructions.

As it happened, James, having heard I would be here through police communications, had also arranged to stay at the Y, and we repaired to our separate rooms to don the necessary costumes— sneakers, shorts, tee shirts, gloves, all the necessaries a handball player never travels without. Then we met on the seventh floor and unlocked a connecting door between the residential and the athletic sections of the complex. This brought us into a large, dimly-lit gymnasium, and from there we found our way down to the fourth floor handball courts.

I must say that I was not impressed with New York's version of an appropriate arena for combat. James was also disappointed. We were accustomed to playing with four walls at our own Y, or three on the L Street beach, but this was a one-wall court. We said nothing, however, no doubt assuming the disadvantage would be the same for both of us.

I must digress here for a moment to tell you something about handball, assuming you do not know the game. The ball is served by hand against a wall, and it bounces back, whereupon it is hit against the wall by the opponent. Each player must hit the ball so that it bounces back within certain boundaries. The players alternate serves every five times, and only the server can make points, when his opponent misses or hits the ball outside the boundaries. If the server does this he has merely lost a chance to make a point.

Other fanatics of the game—and there is no handball player who is not a fanatic—will probably agree with me that a part of the game's fascination is in the absence of paddles, racquets and other tools for hitting the ball. The challenge here is physically direct in that one's hand hits the ball, a gloved hand and a hard rubber ball. Some can play without gloves, but not for long. There is power in the game. The ball can come toward you at an incredible speed. The force of your blow increases the degree of contact. This alone suggests the game's utility for the harmless release of hostilities. I believe it is a factor that keeps the Boston IRA from becoming destructive.

Frequently there occurs between opponents a kind of physical tournament comparable to boxing, except the blows are directed toward the ball rather than each other.

The game can also become, in the absence of hostilities, a battle with oneself. Handball can be a device for objectifying one's frustrations, allowing the mind to relax and find solutions, the barriers to which have been knocked down through the effigy of the handball. There are infinite psychological aspects to the game, but there is no need to go into any more of them at this time. The point is that, in my case, handball that day in New York was as beneficial to me as eight hours of sleep. It allowed me to take my mind off the murders and concentrate on the more controllable logistics of the ball. It was a tremendous release, and I scored point after point.

Once I had achieved a certain amount of mental peace, I began to notice the way James was playing... with a vengeance. He was putting every ounce of that muscular, working class stock into hitting that small rubber ball. He used more force than skill, as though releasing an enormous pent-up emotion. By the end of the game, he was beginning to use his intelligence. But by then it was too late to win, and not too late for a conscious awareness of the shame of his defeat.

"B'jaisus!" he laughed. "I'm not up to my usual excellence, and you seem to have gotten some."

"It's a bad court," I said, trying to help him save face.

"Well, bad or good, I'm still buying," he solved the situation.

If James had anything he wished to alleviate from his mind, he postponed the opportunity by inviting the desk clerk to join us. O'Brien accepted. Therefore, more or less at peace with the world, freshly showered and changed, James and I accompanied O'Brien to a bar whose name (Blarney Stone) and proximity appealed to us.

"We've got a lot of celebrities who use our Y," O'Brien told us and began a respectable list. "And, oh yeah," he remembered, "you guys see the papers, that Peter Piper guy who got killed? He was a member, too. But that wasn't his *real* name."

"Does the name Jerome Lamphere ring a bell?" I asked him.

"Sure, he belonged. I wouldn't call him a celebrity, but he came with Peter Piper sometimes. In fact, Piper brought this Lamphere in during one of our membership drives. We have a couple every year. For every one of your candidates who actually joins, you get a chance for some prize in the membership sweepstakes. Piper didn't win a prize. I would've remembered that."

"Did Lamphere win any prizes?" I asked him.

"Not eligible that time. Next time, yeah, I think he did submit a name, but I don't think anything ever came of it. Anyway, he never won a prize, if that's what you're asking. I'd remember that."

"Do you remember the name he submitted?"

"I'm not the greatest on names. It was a girl, I think."

"Martha Simms?"

"Doesn't ring a bell. If you're interested, we probably got a record. Sometimes we follow up on those names after the membership drives. Drop by the desk, and we'll see." He glanced nervously at the clock. "Are either of you gentlemen blessed with the challenge of wedlock?"

"Is the Pope Catholic?" asked James.

"Then you'll understand why I have to be leaving you," said O'Brien, "though I expect to see you from time to time during your stay."

We assured him that we would, and he weaved his way out of the barroom.

"Nice fella," said James. "Why were you asking him those questions?"

"Oh, just trying to get a clear picture," I said.

"Did you?"

"It just goes more out of focus," I confessed. "My dear friends, Jerome and Doris, I'm not even sure I knew who they were. I wonder if either of them was anything I thought. I can't remember right now the shape of Jerome's nose, or how Doris parted her hair."

"I understand that right enough," said James. "But it's natural, you know. When we're close to someone, maybe we never do know their features. We just think we do. It's the soul we're acquainted with, and that's nothing you can see or describe." That seemed a profound thing for James to be saying, but he followed with, "One of the instructors at the police academy had a theory that if you wanted an accurate description, you'd be better off asking a stranger than a relative. I don't know. I think there might be something to it. Anyway, let's drink to the idea." He signalled for two more. "I suppose you'll be wanting to ask *me* some questions."

"I didn't want to encourage any breach of ethics. I know the police are traditionally very secretive about the facts of a case like this."

"Well," he said, "that's usually the case. But you are the exception that proves the rule. You seem to have earned the tentative trust of one Sergeant Holliman, and I have been instructed to pick your brain if, in my opinion, it's appropriate."

"Pick away," I smiled. "But I thought *I* was going to ask the questions."

"Maybe you should. I'm not even sure what the questions are. It's so bloody confusing." He pulled a notebook from his breast pocket and referred to it. "Here are some things which might help to blur up the picture a little more. Further results of autopsy; Lamphere died from bullet wound."

"I knew that."

"But you didn't know they found traces of poison in his bloodstream."

"No! What kind? The same kind...?"

"Likely."

"Was there alcohol in the bloodstream?"

"I don't have that. The stomach was empty. The bullet was at eight o'clock, so whoever shot him had to be above him and right close."

"Like Jerome was kneeling."

"Or outside a window or something. Now, here's a really interesting thing: lividity."

"Pardon?"

"Lamphere was found on your bed face down. But the blood in his body had settled near his back. Blood doesn't go up after a person is killed. Gravity takes over."

"What does that mean?"

"Guess."

"That he was put on the bed *after* he was killed."

"And probably some time after," said James replacing his notebook in his pocket.

"Was Doris moved?"

"No. And another thing, someone picked up your music manuscript." He paused for effect.

"Who?" I obliged him.

"The garbage man," he said. "Our faithful watchdog got caught napping. He watched the garbage man come and pick up the cans. He watched the garbage man go. Then he looked back where he was supposed to have been looking, and the manuscript was gone. It was chewed up by the truck by the time our man got to the street." The waiter brought our drinks. "Ah, thank you, landlord," James told him, "and have one on us for your own soul's sake."

"That I will," said the waiter who instantly got into the spirit of things, "and God bless you."

"If God can bless a fornicator," said James morosely into his glass after the waiter had left. "I slept with Dorie, Martin. I broke my marriage vows, God forgive me."

"When?" I asked, unable to conceal my astonishment. Then I realized what an odd question that was at a time like this. "I mean," I babbled, "I don't see when you had an opportunity."

"You'll hate me," he said, his Irish cop fading away.

"No!" I protested.

"Well, it was some Thursday evenings when I *wasn't* directing traffic at Fenway Park, those evenings when you would be out with Doctor Sterne."

I did not need to ask him where.

"Were you with her," I fumbled, hoping he would not read any Biblical connotations into that, "... with her last Thursday?"

"That time I *was* directing traffic," he said, "and that is the very time I should have been with her." And he began to cry.

"Forgive me, James, but do you think she came there that night to meet you?"

"No," he sobbed. "She knew. We were going to spend Monday night together, instead, after she left work."

"We will talk more of this at *another* time," I said finally.

"Yes," he agreed, when he had partially recovered his manly demeanor. "Yes, another time, Martin me boy."

We were silent.

"I didn't come here to tell you that," he said after a while, taking a huge gulp of his drink and signalling for two more. I started to protest and then caught myself, for my protestations, besides being in bad taste, would have broken the spell. I decided to submit to one drink too many.

"I was sent here," he said finally. "I was sent here by that devil Holliman. I am 'implicated', as the good Sergeant put it, in the dreadful goings-on of Thursday. I am temporarily, therefore, suspended from the force until it's all solved and I am cleared of blame."

"You were permitted to leave Boston?"

"I was instructed to remove my face from the Sergeant's sight and work on the case from this end, cooperating of course with the locals." He sighed and drank. Than he drank and sighed. "Oh, there's no denying I have personal reasons for wanting to see the culprit hanged, preferably by me... although I'd be happy to share the honor with yourself, providing you can beat me once more at handball. You see, I neglected to return the key to O'Brien."

"God bless you," I said, and we raised aloft our one-drinks-too-many and downed them before we thought to taste or swallow. And soon, arm in arm, we were swaying back to the Y for an improbable game. Soon we were once again hitting that small rubber ball wherever it chose to go.

"She was truly a lovely woman, was Dorie," he said, taking his fifth serve.

"That she was," I said as it bounced and I returned it low to the floor. My serve. "I knew her, you know, since college. A spirited girl then."

"Ah yes, spirited. She didn't lose that, Martin me boy, she only hid it. But it was there. It was still there." The return was beyond my reach. He was playing a better game now.

"How do you know?" I asked, taking my second serve.

"She had dreams, Martin. She made me dream, God rest her soul." No point. "And how could some blackhearted rogue take that away from her?" he asked slapping the ball out of bounds. My point.

"We'll get him, James. We'll get him." We lost the ball, but found it with some difficulty in an unexplainable shadow on the court. I put the ball back into play.

"We know... I know... and now I'm telling you..." he slapped it hard, and for a moment all we could think about was the game. This was the longest volley, back and forth, return, return, until finally I lost the point and the serve. He laughed loud and long, and I joined him. He served.

"What was I sayin'?"

I really couldn't remember.

"Oh yes. The gun. The gun that waylaid poor Jerry Jerome."

"What about it?" I asked, missing my return.

"You lost that one, Martin me boy," he crowed.

As is customary, I examined my glove for defects. Then we played some more.

Several points later, an image slowly crept through my drunken haze... gun. "Gun!" I shouted, and he lost a point.

"Ah, so it's that kind of game we're playin', is it?"

We played some more until finally he asked the inevitable question, "What's the score?"

I didn't know. "I don't know."

"Who's winning?" he demanded.

I really didn't know. "I am," I said. "One more point and it's my game."

Accustomed to losing to me as he was, he accepted my statement. Now I brought every ounce of concentration I could muster to the game. It was precious little, but we were once again playing with similar handicaps. I am clear on only one fact of our game. I did win the last point, and right or wrong, that did make me the winner. After he missed an easy bounce off the wall, he stood there on the court, stooped like an idiot, his jaw hanging slack. He was silent for a moment in this foolish posture.

"Beat me square and fair," he said and began to sing...

"Fare thee well my lady
Farewell, my own true love..."

then forgetting the words, "Then what?"

"I don't know," I said.

"Whadaya mean? You're a scholar, a musicologist, aren't you? Whadaya mean, you don't know?"

Fare thee well, my lady!!
Farewell, my own true love!!

THEN WHAT?! " he shouted.

I made something up and sang off-key,

"Until they hang me high-dee,
you'll be my turtle dove."

"That's right!" he said and repeated,

"Until they hang me high-dee,
You'll be my turtle dove..."

His voice trailed off, and arm in arm we proceeded to the elevator. "You're a good man. Martin me boy," he said.

As we returned to our rooms, we sang in verbal unity and dual pitches:

"Fare thee well, my lady.
Farewell, my own true love.
Until they hang me high-dee,
You'll be my turtle dove."

We arrived at my room. "Won't you come in?" I asked.

"After you," he gestured.

"No, no," I protested, "after *you*."

"B'jaisus, Martin, you won the bloody game, and now I'm tellin' you, 'After *YOU!*'"

"Right enough," I said and preceeded him into the room.

There happened to be two beds in my room, and he

plopped down on one of them as I did likewise on the other.

"You ought to take a shower and get in your pajamas," he said, "just as I intend to."

"You're right," I said without moving.

There was a moment of silence, and then he started giggling, which set me off. Another silence. Then the whole thing started over again. Finally exhausted from our laughter, we started to go to sleep. Only vaguely do I recall in the moments before Morpheus finally claimed me, a voice which sounded very much like James' voice at a slower speed saying, "Oh, yes, the gun... The third fingerprint... belonged to someone named Harold Hauser."

"Peter Piper," I think I answered.

"Tha's right," I think he said.

I descended abruptly into a deep and dreamless sleep.

Chapter XIV

I would not say I felt unwell the next morning, only that I was apprehensive about feeling unwell. Of course, I was accustomed to living on the edge of chaos, but this time I felt much less capable of coping with the situation should it become worse. I was afraid to get out of bed.

I had been awakened by the lonely squeal of a masticating garbage truck. The sound rolled around the empty caverns of my head. As a kind of centrifugal reaction to this, my eyes rolled to the left and seemed to fall like two marbles on the empty bed next to me. This exertion promised nausea, so I lay frozen as I sent out mental trouble-shooters to check out the damage to the interior of my hull. After a suspended moment, they returned to report I would never sail again.

Ah well, I philosophized to myself, at least one last look through a window. Without my blessings, my body rose from the bed, picked up my eyeballs and transported me to the window.

Outside, Twenty-third Street looked as though it had been washed with bright gray water. I blinked, swept aside the improbable piece of dyed burlap which curtained the window, and then the brightness and the heat hit me like ball lightning and sent me reeling backward onto the bed. I felt as though I had seen the angry features of The Great Librarian.

Any thought of going back to sleep was unreasonably rejected by the persistent alarm of my inner clock. So I arose again, found my way outside to the w.c., performed certain ablutions, then left, greeting a familiar nausea beyond the room's tiled security.

On a couple of occasions I had been present to "assist" Jerome when he felt as I did. Doris and I once propelled him to the bathroom with verbal images of liver sauteed in chocolate. The memory was ill-advised, for although it sent me speeding back to the w.c., the stomach was ultimately stronger than the image. I resigned myself to a day of great physical uncertainty.

I dressed in slow motion, found my way down the elevator to the lobby and dutifully left my key at the desk. After all, why should the Y be inconvenienced should I never return to my room? A message was waiting for me at the desk.

Martin, my boy!!—got an idea and had to go out. Didn't want to wake you, and don't think I could have anyway. I'll be finding you later. How's your Irish head? Hair of the dog— Jimmy O.

The sun was brutal outside as it had been through my window. I reasoned that its punishment must be good for me and decided to walk the fifteen blocks uptown to Martha's office. No sooner had I committed myself than I regretted it.

The sounds of the city were louder than normal, it seemed, even though I had managed to sleep through the early rush hour. Why could I not have as easily committed myself to spending my recovery in the Y's sauna?

The office of Borman Publications squatted in a building with a respectable lobby and a respectable elevator that deposited one at a variety of environments. The eleventh floor, in contrast to some of the others, had hallway walls ignored by graffitoists and unloved by everyone else. The ceiling had that kind of metal design one associates with condemned buildings. The door of Borman Publications was a mahogany counterfeit with a small brass plate which seemed to attempt contradiction of its environment. This door, perhaps, protected roses from the weed patch.

As I opened the door, I was greeted by another, shorter, hallway, designed, it seemed, for the sole purpose of displaying the most lurid and striking art from recent Borman magazine covers.

"Hi there. Can I help you?" asked a voice from behind a window-like opening at one end. I stepped over and looked below the sill. A matronly lady turned away from reading galleys and gave me her receptionist smile. Then it vanished as she became suspicious. "You the new writer?"

"I'm Martin Webb, a friend of Martha Simms."

"Oh," she said, and she gestured with her grease pencil toward a door at the other end of the short hallway. "Right in there."

I entered the office she had indicated. It held four desks, several filing cabinets, a television set, a small refrigerator—a kind of blissful hodgepodge which might give one an historical perspective if he had the patience to create order from it. Men sat at two of the desks, one typing, one on the phone. A third desk was being cleaned out by Martha, a task she was performing with furious determination. She got up from her work and came to me as I entered.

"Martin, how are you?" she asked with more concern than etiquette.

"Fine," I said automatically. "So this is where you work."

"Yes," she said, "but you've caught me doing a different kind of job. We think we'll have a new writer here soon," she explained grimly. "So I volunteered to perform these... necessary rites."

The drawers of the desk were open and seemingly empty. On the top were scattered a couple of pipes, some book matches, some medicinal mints in individual cellophane wrappings, a portable typewriter and some manuscripts, one of which Martha used to fan herself. "Some of his old articles," she said, "but not the novel."

"I suppose we'll never know what that was all about," I suggested.

"No," she agreed. "He hardly ever talked about his stuff while he was working on it, so in a way he took the novel with him."

"But I think he did intend to discuss it with me, and we have reason to believe he discussed it with Harold."

"Not with me," she said, slamming a drawer. Then she turned to the man who was hanging up the telephone receiver. "It's ready when you are," she said with finality and dropped the manuscripts into a wastebasket.

"Thanks, kid," he said. "Preciate it." He was a tall, young man wearing a bright wide tie, an oval head with tinted glasses and a crew cut.

"This is Mr. Bob," Martha introduced him. "Mr. Bob, Martin Webb, the friend of Jerry's I told you about."

"Greetings," said Mr. Bob.

"How do you do . . ." I began.

"Call me Mr. Bob," he interrupted. "It's my nickname. The real one is Andrew Roberts. But everyone needs a nickname, right? Besides, in our business *nom de plumes* are useful. For instance, this incompetent over here goes under the alias of Liza Merriweather." He gestured magnanimously to the other gentleman, a short, dark young man who cleverly concealed a missing tooth with a Glenn Ford grin.

"It's a pen name," explained Liza, grinning. Now that he had Mr. Bob's attention, he asked, "How about this?" and read from his typewriter, "The Home of Hollywood's Secret Love Cult—Where Beast Meets Beast." He looked up. "Do you love it?"

"I love it," said Mr. Bob, "but not a lot."

"Just give me a chance, chief," said Liza ripping the page from his typewriter and inserting another. "I know I can make good."

"Want a coke or something?" Mr. Bob asked me as he opened the refrigerator.

"I do," said Liza and got one.

I declined. "Does anyone here know about Jerome?" I asked Martha quietly.

"Jerome!" Mr. Bob picked up the cue. "Jerry."

Liza stopped typing, making a silence which he soon broke. "Who's going to write the nostalgia piece on Alice Faye?" he seemed to ask his typewriter.

"You see that desk?" Mr. Bob pointed to the one Martha had emptied. "In a few days it will be occupied again because it has to be, because life goes on. There will be somebody else to write about Alice Faye. It won't be the same. It won't be one of those great Jerry Lamphere ideas that I just loved. We're all sorry he's gone from us. But we have to go on." There was a pause until Liza's typewriter tentatively resumed its background noise. "What can I do?" Mr. Bob asked. "I'd like to do something for Jerry."

"How about this?" asked Liza looking up from his typewriter. "Hollywood Erotica—A Fancy Word for a Primitive Rite. Do you love it?"

"I love it," said Mr. Bob. "Can you make it more earthy?"

"Right, Chief!"

"Now," said Mr. Bob, "what can we do?"

"There's a kind of celebration," Martha said.

"A celebration?"

"I know it sounds weird, but it's sort of right. You remember Empie and Boris, the place where Jerry stayed when he first came to the city? They're having a party in Jerry's honor. You could come to that."

Mr. Bob's eyebrows raised, then lowered, and he smiled. "I love it. I'd be happy to come."

"Can I come, too?" asked Liza, still typing.

"May he come, too?" asked Mr. Bob.

"Of course," said Martha.

"Anything else?" Mr. Bob asked me. "I mean, besides gracing the post mortem with my presence."

"I'd be curious to know," I said, "if you can remember anything in particular about that last day you saw Jerome."

"I remember *everything* in particular, perhaps nothing Martha hasn't already told you, but let's see..." He strolled to the window behind his desk and looked out at the brick wall facing him, then he turned back to us. "Jerry arrived a few minutes early that day. It was his habit to be ahead of schedule when the day promised to be unusual in any way. I was the only one here when he walked in carrying that typewriter—he took it back and forth—" He pointed to the machine on the unoccupied desk, "and his brown duffle bag and a manila envelope containing his novel."

"Are you certain it was the novel?"

"Quite certain," he said. "But suppose I take the details in their proper order."

"Of course."

"...Carrying a brown duffle bag—L.L. Bean, I think—and a loose-leaf notebook containing his novel, about a hundred pages, I would judge by the bulk. He put it down on his desk there and, after a few amenities of no consequence, proceeded to work. Martha came in promptly as the clock was striking nine— I say that figuratively since no clocks strike here. She handed him the car keys, kissed him lightly on the head where his hair was growing thin, and then she, too, proceeded to work. The morning was without incident, just the happy clacking away of typewriters, music to my ears. He paused to listen whimsically to Liza's typewriter.

"There..." he lowered his voice and nodded toward

Liza, "you hear the sound of an ignorant genius. He gets stuck on titles, but once he gets started on a story, he can turn out the inspired drivel we publish at an average seventy words a minute without ever looking back. He is a treasure. Martha types with the professional objectivity of a trained secretary. Jerry, though, was a creature of moods, subject to the artistic despair of one who coveted the Pulitzer Prize. His typewriter was halting, frustrated, tormented. I only tell you this to point out the contrast in what his typewriter told me on Thursday. On that day it was practically humming with creativity, peace and joy.

"The morning progressed in this way until we went to lunch. We often ate together at a little coffee shop around the corner, Martha and Jerry and I. On Thursday, as we waited to cross the street toward the restaurant I noticed the car—gray BMW—on the other side, and I complimented Martha on finding such a convenient parking place. Some children were just beginning to write dubious phrases in the dust on the side of the car when Jerry yelled at them. They left, verbally assaulting us with some of the things they didn't get a chance to write. I asked Martha at that point if a car as dirty as hers might not be banned in Boston. But Jerry pledged a clean car when he returned."

"Which side of the car were you looking at then?" I asked.

"The driver's side."

"There's so little chance of getting a car clean in the city," said Martha.

"And so little *point*," Mr. Bob added. "At any rate, Jerry who was normally disturbed by dirt, was not bothered this time. In encouragement from Martha, he decided to forgo his usually cautious diet and have a hot roast beef sandwich with gravy and mashed potatoes."

"I'm afraid I did encourage him," Martha admitted. "I loved to watch him eat when he was happy."

"Then," Mr. Bob told her, "you should have stuck around for the pie. He truly tore into that."

This talk of food began to affect me, and my nausea must have been evident.

"Perhaps a Lamphere special," Mr. Bob suggested to Martha. She nodded, scooped something from the top of Jerome's desk and went outside with it. "This is just like last Thursday," Mr. Bob said, "with you playing the part of Jerry. Shall we wait?"

"No," I protested bravely, "please go on."

"Of course," Mr Bob continued, "I had known previously that Jerry was writing a novel. *I* am writing a novel. My dental hygienist is writing a novel. Practically everyone I know, except Liza, is writing a novel. At any rate, in the sense of brotherhood which often follows a meal, I felt akin to Jerry as another novelist, and I asked to know more about his project. But this time he turned the conversation around to me. He asked me what motive *I* might have for killing him. Isn't that interesting?"

"What did you tell him?"

He sat in the swivel chair behind his desk and leaned toward me. "I was not coy," he said. "I knew it was a first novel, after all, and unlikely to be published. So when he asked me why I might kill him, I told him. I'd doubt he couldn't have figured it out by himself. I said my motive was jealousy. How, he asked a little too tritely, could I be jealous of *him*? After all, I had a wife and children and an expensive house in Queens. How could I be jealous of him?"

"I was jealous, I told him, *because* I had a wife and children and an expensive house. My livelihood, and the mortgage on that house, was dependent on manufacturing fantasies day after day for people to whom houses in Queens were fantasies. I secretly hated and coveted the lives of the Jerry's of the world. They had wrenched their freedom from life as I did not dare to. They worked for me, for wages, but they weren't committed to my way of life. They used me, as it were, to live my own fantasies. I could never do what Jerry was doing. I had lost the vision I once had and which Jerry had now and which he was using me to support. I was jealous because I was supporting my fantasy in someone else. Why would I kill Jerry? Because he dared to try to be what I once thought I was. Is that clear? Do you understand?"

His monologue ended, Mr. Bob swiveled his chair toward the window and looked out. Martha returned with a glass of something that fizzed. For a moment, I had forgotten my own condition but was now reminded. "A few quick gulps," she prescribed, "then sip the rest." She watched me gulp and sip. "Sometimes it helps," she said. "If it doesn't, you can come to my place. I'll make you a cup of Empie's tea. Or she'll make you some at her place tonight."

I weakly smiled my thanks. "Her place . . . tonight?"

"Had you forgotten?" I had. "You don't have to go."

"May we wait and see?" I asked. She nodded and I turned to Mr. Bob. "Was there anything else?" I asked. "I mean, after lunch?"

"We returned to the office," he said dully, still looking out the window. "Unlike the morning, Jerry's typewriter sounded more thoughtful. But he worked continuously and in silence until 3:30 when he went to the men's room. He returned, worked a bit more slowly, until it was 4:15. He admitted he wasn't feeling well, so Martha brought him one of those seltzer drinks. Then he left work early, with my permission. Martha called us to the window to watch him drive away. Was the car behaving strangely, she wanted to know. It was not. And he was gone."

"I've got it," Liza broke in. "I've got it all! The title, the angle and most of the story."

"May Maurice Zolotow grant you further wisdom," said Mr. Bob.

Hollywood Erotica...A fancy Word for an Earthy Rite'" Liza read from his typewriter. "'The Strange Cults of the Sex Stars'...that's the title. Do you love it?"

"I love it," said Mr. Bob looking out the window. "I love it a lot."

Chapter XV

I thought it wise to return to the Y, lie down quietly and see if a few things would not fall into place. Upon arriving, I went to the desk to retrieve my key and to see if James had left me some new message. O'Brien was at the desk and greeted me somewhat coldly, I thought, considering our fellowship of the previous evening.

"Any messages for...?"

"No, none!" he cut me off and busied himself with papers.

"You do remember...?" I tried to reassert myself in his memory.

"I remember you! You're the one who sneaks into handball courts after hours." His eyes rolled significantly to the right. It became transparently clear that he was trying to warn me about a young man who was leaning on one end of the counter and watching us. He looked like a tall pixie, I thought, and wore a lightweight seersucker suit, a floral sportshirt and a handlebar moustache. There seemed to be nothing threatening about him. O'Brien, in case I misunderstood his warnings, prompted me further. "I've a good mind to turn you in to this officer, if he didn't have more important business. But you'd better go about *your* business before I change my mind," he suggested and pointed toward the elevator, a gesture more of pleading than dismissal.

"Sneaking into handball courts, the idea!" said the young man flashing his badge. "May I see your identification?"

"I was just havin' some fun with Sammy here," O'Brien told him. "Is there no sense of humor in the police force anymore?"

101

"Your identification?" the man repeated.

"The jig appears to be up," I explained to O'Brien and dutifully removed my wallet which I opened to my driver's license.

"H. Martin Webb?" asked the man. "The 'H'... I suppose that stands for Sammy."

"A typographical error?" I suggested.

"I don't think so," he said. "I've been waiting here for an H. Martin Webb, Sammy, and since you happen to have his driver's license, I suggest you come with me."

"Don't you have to read him something?" asked O'Brien.

"I'll read *you*!" said the man.

"Something about having the right to remain silent and so forth?" persisted O'Brien.

"You've been watching too much television," the man suggested. "Will you come along peacefully?" he asked me, his tone of voice seeming to suggest that it would be a good idea.

"He didn't *really* sneak into the handball court," was the only remaining straw onto which O'Brien was able to clutch, as I was ushered out the door.

"You may be in serious trouble," said the man as we emerged onto the hot, bright street.

"Is it permitted to ask why?"

"Very serious," he said as we moved toward a parked car. "There was a murder in Brooklyn this afternoon..." he paused, turned and stared at me accusingly, "and *you weren't there!*"

"I beg your pardon?"

"You *are* the Boston H. Martin Webb who discovered two bodies in his own apartment?"

"Yes."

"Who thereupon came to this city to discover yet another body?"

"Well...yes...."

"And you were, you claim, innocent on both occasions?"

"Yes."

"Well, if you are innocent of deaths at which you are present, doesn't it follow that you should be suspect by your absence in Brooklyn today? What do you say to that?"

I had nothing to say, absolutely nothing. Then the situation was mercifully explained by loud laughter which came from the nearby car, and a face poked out the window. It was O'Toole.

"Had you going there a minute, didn't we?" asked the man and gave me a friendly thump on the shoulder. "Come on. Get in."

"He's a joker, that Bimbo," laughed O'Toole as I got into the back seat of the car. "Martin, meet Bimbo Schwartz."

"How do you do?" I said doubtfully.

"How can you be a cop in this town without a sense of humor?" explained Bimbo.

"What do you think?" James asked me while gesturing to Bimbo. "What do you think of a guy this young, probably with a moustache he had to paste on, that young he is...already risen to the ranks of junior detective...growin' blisters on his butt that should be on his feet from walking a beat? What do you think of all that, Martin me boy? Can you tell me what this world is coming to?"

"Well, I'm not thinking too clearly right now," I said, trying to retain my sense of direction as the car moved downtown, I thought toward the Greenwich Village area.

"Being from Boston," said Bimbo, "you wouldn't know. The whole program's been stepped up to attract go-get-'em types like Batman and Robin and me."

103

"Okay," said James, "let's go get 'em then."

"*Where* are we going?" I asked, "and also, *why?*"

"Well, you see, Martin," said James, "when I woke up this morning, you were dead to the world, and that got a train of thought going through my fuzzy head. I thought of 'dead to the world,' and then I thought of 'dead,' and that made me think of Harold Hauser, his fingerprint on the gun and all, and that made me decide to go check out his apartment."

"They caught him trying to break in," said Bimbo.

"But after the appropriate introductions," said James, "showing of badges..."

"Secret handshakes..." said Bimbo.

"The usual. And after I had convinced them of the purity of my intentions, and after they had chided me for not checking in with them first—because the good Sergeant Holliman had been asking after me and they didn't know what to tell him and were quite upset, it being long distance and the taxpayer's dollar and all—after the chiding, they let me into the apartment and showed me the sights. And after *that* I knew as much as I did before."

"You found out about Hauser's background," Bimbo prompted him.

"From you guys, not from the apartment."

"What background?" I asked. "His film career?"

"No," said Bimbo. "He had an old record for burglary. Got caught a couple of times, so there might've been a hundred times he got away with it."

"True," said James. "And I found out Jerry smoked marijuana." He turned to me and asked, "Did you know that?"

"No," I said. "It's difficult to believe."

"Well," said James, "one of his pipes was obviously used for that purpose. But it's no great matter, Martin. Not in this day and age."

"What were you looking for?" I asked.

"Maybe another gun," said James, "one that worked, not those rusty relics in the bedroom. I'm not sure. It's a dumb case, so you can't expect being logical is going to get us anywhere."

"Dumb is right," agreed Bimbo. "All the fingerprints belong to dead people."

James turned to me. "And *one* side of the car was clean. Why? To erase the fingerprints of someone who isn't dead? From *one side*?"

"Both sides were dirty that afternoon," I said. "I found that out from Jerome's employer."

"So somewhere between New York and Boston, one side of the car got washed."

"One of my musical manuscripts was taken," I offered. "The least valuable one."

"And what do all these dumb things tell us?" asked James.

"That the criminal was stupid?" I wondered.

"That there was someone stupid in your apartment that night," said James.

"Or," I suggested, "it might be that these facts which seem stupid have some logic we haven't yet found."

"We're making real progress," said Bimbo.

"Speaking of that," I asked, "where are we going?"

"Oh yes," said James. "We're going try to trace the gun, and I wanted you along because you talked to Hauser before he died. You might think of the right questions. But I can't, and won't, force you to go with us, Martin. We may in fact, be about to enter onto a scene too horrible for you to contemplate, and you may want to just stay in the car. After all, police work is a special kind of work. We are trained in dealing with the dark side of life. The blood and the gore of it are nothing more to us than the notes on a sheet of music to you."

"For heaven's sake," I asked, "where are we going?"

"Where they make dirty movies," said Bimbo twirling his moustache.

James became serious. "Okay?"

I hesitated, certainly not looking forward to the experience. "I shall try," I said.

"Staunch fellow," said Bimbo as he brought the car to a halt in front of an orange warehouse in an alley somewhere in Greenwich Village. "Dirty movie place!" he announced. "Everybody out!"

Chapter XVI

"This was one of the places we raided when the courts cracked down on the pornos," said Bimbo as we proceeded upward to the third landing. "We're pretty good friends now."

A small name tape over a bell button said "Bingham." Bimbo rang the bell. There was a click behind the door as someone lifted an unseen peephole cover, after which the door promptly opened.

"Heighdy, Bimbo," said a rather plump, rather young blonde with traces of acne. "Heighdy! Who'd you bring?"

"Chicken," said Bimbo, "these are some dirty old men from Boston."

"They don't get any dirtier than that," she giggled.

Bimbo turned to us. "This young lady is billed as Chicken Coquette."

"Come on in," she said opening the door, revealing herself to be naked before I had time to lower my gaze. "It's very hot in here," she said. I could hear her padding from us toward another door. "Make yourselves as comfortable as you can, and I'll ask Michael if he's in." The apparition vanished, discreetly closing the door behind her.

"Jaisus!" said James to fill the silence which followed her departure.

"She's really a very nice girl," said Bimbo.

"I can see that," said James.

The room we were in contained a couple of sofas, a desk, many theatrical photographs, a few posters— among them the "Peter Piper in *Bad Guy*" I had noticed in Harold's room— and a dartboard. We sat down and waited to see if Michael was in.

"Have you gotten to know her very well?" James, who could not get his mind off our reception, asked Bimbo.

"Well, if you call arresting her once or twice knowing her well...." said Bimbo, his voice trailing off. "I've seen three of her movies," he added. "Two of them in the line of duty."

"Then she's an actress," I tried to hold my own.

"Well," said Bimbo, "she's in movies, you know?"

"Isn't she afraid of being arrested again?" asked James.

"No," said Bimbo. "She's not doing anything wrong anymore."

Further conversation was squelched by the entrance of a dour young man in bathing trunks. "What do you want, Bimbo?" he asked with the tone of someone perpetually martyred. "Haven't you done enough?" And he sank disconsolately into the sofa opposite us.

"Michael," said Bimbo, "meet Jimmy O'Toole of the Boston police force."

"I don't know anybody in Boston," Michael said quickly.

"...and his friend, Martin Webb."

"What do you do?" he asked me suspiciously.

"I'm a librarian," I simplified the explanation.

"So what's up?" Michael asked Bimbo gloomily. "If you're giving these guys a tour at my expense, there's nothing particularly interesting to look at anymore. Even had to sell our air conditioning to pay the fine."

"Now, now," said Bimbo. "You're better off than most people in your business. You've got your own place, your own equipment, and you're not being exploited by the Mafia."

"Some comfort," said Michael. "Look. The cops have already been here about Harold. I couldn't tell them anymore than you read in the papers." He shook his head. "Too——bad. He was good. It's a real loss to the industry. Was it suicide, or what?"

"We don't know," Bimbo lied. "Why?"

"He got depressed enough to do it sometimes," said Michael. "But I don't think he'd want to do anything unless he could be around to see its effect. A real actor!"

"He worked for you?" asked James.

"Yeah, in my A Unit. We had an agreement he wouldn't work for anybody else, and I gave him a good deal. Why shouldn't I? I discovered him."

"Mind telling our visitors how you did that?" asked Bimbo.

Michael sighed as one accustomed to such police games. "I caught him robbing this place," he said in a monotone. "I knew he was an actor right off. Here he was looking for loose change in my dump, but he was acting like a famous, international jewel thief. A real actor. Well, I was short an actor, so I told him if he'd do it, I wouldn't turn him in. He did it. Boy, did he do it! He was good. And he never had to rob anybody after that." He rolled his head languidly to Bimbo. "Did I leave anything out?"

"No, said Bimbo. "Relax."

Michael sighed again. "It's lucky we didn't get a new project started with the A Unit yet."

"Why's that?" asked James.

"Well, we'd have to go back and reshoot all Harold's scenes with somebody else to finish the film."

"Did you have one planned?"

"Yeah, that's what I mean. We were scheduled to start filming last Thursday, but we had to call it off. We were having trouble with the sound man. And then Harold couldn't make it, either. I was mad then, at both of them, but I guess it was a lucky thing."

"Did Harold have any enemies?" asked James.

"None I know of," said Michael, then nodded toward Bimbo, "present company excepted."

"How did he get along with his roommate?"

"Look. Did he mention me or anybody before he kicked off?"

"I may have been the last person to see him alive," I said. "He only mentioned his roommate, Jerome Lamphere."

"He was always talking about Jerry," said Michael. "Seemed to like him fine. Wanted him to write a movie for us." A noise behind the door attracted his attention for a moment. "Look. We're kind of busy today. It's the B Unit, and most of them are pretty new. You here to question people, or what? Because the B Unit hardly knew Harold."

"We're trying to trace a gun," said Bimbo, "a pistol."

"What can I tell you?"

"We think it might have come from here."

"Well...." Michael looked anxiously toward the door, then back. "We do have some props here. Nobody watches them very closely. I think there was a gun. We might've used one in a couple of films. I don't know if it shot anything but blanks."

"May we see it?" asked James.

"Suppose it wasn't registered? Is it against the law to show it?"

"It's against the law if you don't," said Bimbo.

Michael looked particularly depressed. "Coming or going," he muttered. "Got you both ways." He opened the inner door and fatalistically gestured for us to follow him. In the next room, seated at a table and framed in a pool of light, were a man and woman staring strangely at a rubber glove which seemed to be moving. "Science fiction," explained Michael. "Watch out for that cable."

We gingerly picked our way among half-seen cables, going slowly until our eyes became accustomed to the darkness. Then it became apparent that the crew was in various stages of undress. Michael saw my expression as I looked away. "It's hot work," he explained. "I feel sorry for those poor actors sweating in those costumes. It wasn't always this tough for them, before the raids. This way."

He led us into another room and closed the door. "It might get stifling," he promised as he switched on the overhanging bulb, revealing a small room with a projector facing a piece of white cardboard taped to the opposite wall. On a shelf were film cans, and on other shelves and surfaces were equipment and various paraphernalia which must have been used in Michael Bingham movies.

"I don't see any gun," said Michael looking about the shelves.

"Any pictures of it?" asked Bimbo.

"You know we got pictures," said Michael raising his eyes pleadingly to the ceiling. "Okay. What do you want to see?"

"There was a gun in *Bad Guy*," said Bimbo. "Was that the one?"

"We'll soon see." Michael pulled a film can off the shelf, removed a reel and threaded it onto the projector. "This is a very popular film," he told me. "The judge and jury seemed to find it necessary to see it twice. As far as I'm concerned, they were all out for a cheap high at my expense." He turned suddenly on Bimbo. His voice rose with outrage. "*And* at the expense, I might add, of a lot of sincere kids who were just barely making a living as it was and who now have to sweat their tails off out there doing work they don't believe in. You want cheap films, you'll get cheap films. Before we finish with sci-fis, you're going to beg us to go back to making movies like this one."

I must say he had whetted my interest. I had been bracing myself for being subjected to some indecent, immoral, pornographic film, and now I wasn't certain, swayed as I was by Michael's artistic conviction. Seeming to sense a receptive audience in me, he sat beside me as the film began.

There was music of sorts, mostly Congo drums, and then the title *Bad Guy*, followed by a respectable number of credits, including the mention of Peter Piper and Chicken Coquette. "When other people thought they needed a teaser," Michael told me, "*we* were showing clean, white titles on a black background right at the beginning. Now Hollywood's doing it. But we did it first."

He became silent as the action started on the screen. There was Harold fully clothed in blue jeans and leather jacket walking along a street in a rather nice neighborhood. "We went on location for this part," explained Michael, "uptown."

A very tailored woman—Chicken Coquette—passes him walking a small poodle.

"Isn't that the young lady with your *B* Unit?" I asked.

"This was before we had a B Unit," Michael explained.

As Harold's gaze is directed to Chicken, he steps into something on the sidewalk and becomes furious. However, instead of the oaths Harold is apparently preparing to hurl at Chicken and her indiscriminate dog, when he opens his mouth to shout, loud traffic noises emerge.

"What we're saying here," said Michael, "is there's a lot of hostility in the city."

"You're just way ahead of your time," said Bimbo.

Harold was seen wiping his foot on the curb as he watched Chicken Coquette proceed down the street with the dog.

In the next scene, we see Harold entering his room, a very plain and unimaginative environment. He drags a suitcase out from under a bed and searches through it until he finds a gun. He cleans it sensously with a cloth, wiping it clean. Closeup of Harold smiling. Closeup of the gun in Harold's hand. "Hold it there," said Bimbo.

"Okay." said Michael. "We'll put it on the editing machine." He turned off the projector, removed the film and threaded it onto two handled spools which ran the film behind a small lighted screen. We watched as Bimbo found the film frame with the gun.

"It doesn't show up well in that size," said Bimbo. "Is there a better shot?"

"Of course," said Michael, turning the reel furiously. "It's a symbol!"

The figures on the screen moved at an abnormal pace.

Next scene Harold runs jerkily along the nice street with hands in pocket. Again steps on something. "That's for comic relief," explained Michael, "because it gets very heavy in a minute." It was, as a matter of fact, quite funny at the fast speed.

Harold goes up steps to front door. Closeup of his hand holding wire.

Michael now slowed the action, as Harold's hand is shown slowly fitting the wire into the lock. "This is authentic," said Michael. "He really is picking that lock."

After an over-long lock-picking lesson, the scene shifts to the interior. Oddly enough, it looks very much like Harold's room of the previous scene, except there are a few plants scattered about, pictures on the wall and a different covering on the bed.

"We used the same location here for the girl's apartment as we did for the guy's apartment," said Michael, again speeding up the picture. "The point here is, even though her place is a little fancier than his, they're not so different. Get it?"

Harold draws gun. Chicken enters room, dressed as before, neat dark suit and white gloves. She sees Harold, screams.

"More traffic noise there instead of a scream," Michael filled in for the missing sound track. "Emphasis."

Harold threatens Chicken with gun. She pleads. A struggle. She gets the gun away and holds it on him. He is surprised, begins to undress.

"You see what we're doing here?" Michael asked me.

"You're showing that they are the same person?" I ventured looking away.

"I wish you'd been on that jury," said Michael.

The reader will forgive and perhaps thank me if I hereby end my description of the film. That which I saw of the rest was, for all its social content, extremely pornographic, and in fast motion quite ridiculous. Harold, alias Peter Piper, was shown in the passive role Empie mentioned. Chicken Coquette was, from the moment she obtained possession of the gun, in full control of the situation and led Harold into adventures that he ... or the dog ... probably never dreamed of. When I was not looking at the screen, which was often, I was looking at James and Bimbo whose stalwart attention to duty was most commendable, their attention never wavering from their purpose in being there.

I did, at Michael's request, pay close attention to one sequence containing closeups of the gun as Chicken's white-gloved hand put it sensuously into a plastic bag. To my untutored eye, it did indeed seem to be the one I had seen in my bedroom four nights earlier. Appreciative comments from James—I assume about gun—indicated that we were in agreement.

When the film had ended and Michael had switched on the overhead light, I looked shyly at the others. They were all looking shyly at me.

"B'jaisus!" said James. Other than that, we were all strangely silent as Michael rewound the film. This done, Michael asked if we wished to see it again. James and

Bimbo exchanged looks, there was an uncertain pause, and then James said "no" and "thank you."

Michael opened the door for us, and we proceeded across the second room toward the outer office. B Unit had apparently taken a break and was sitting around, two clothed actors and others in various stages of nudity, one wearing a rubber glove. They smiled cheerfully at us as we passed, and we passed in a most business-like manner.

"So was that the gun?" Michael asked as we arrived in the outer room. The rest of us agreed that it was. "Well," he said, "the last time I saw it, it was on that shelf in there, still in the plastic bag you saw it put into in the film. Will this get me into more trouble?" he asked, preparing himself for the worst.

"Not if I can help it," said Bimbo. "How did you edit that film, anyway? What order did you shoot the scenes in?"

"I shoot my scenes in the order you see them," Michael puffed himself up. "My movies are real!" Then he recovered his previous train of thought, his vulnerable pride disappearing, leaving only his vulnerability. "I mean the gun might not be registered. Actually, I think we found it lying around."

"Don't worry about it," said Bimbo. "We never yet shafted anybody for helping us."

"That's real nice," said Michael slowly. "Look, if I've been riding you too hard about the raids and the trial and the air conditioning, I'm sorry. It's just that it's so hot."

"Look on the bright side," said Bimbo. "If we hadn't raided this place, you and I never would've met. And I turned out to be your best fan."

"What would you rather have," James grinned foolishly, "a big fan or a little air conditioner."

"Mr. Bingham," I said, partly to hide the non-response to James' quip, "you mentioned Harold being unable to perform in a film on Thursday. Did he say why he couldn't do it?"

"No," answered Michael. "I asked him, too. He told me he had to go out of town... but I think he was lying."

"Why do you say that?"

"A hunch? I don't know. I knew he had to go away Sunday for a couple of days to do a personal appearance. But this other thing came up at the last minute, and it sounded like a pretty lame excuse to me. When's the funeral?"

I explained that the body was probably still in the morgue.

Michael nodded. "I guess from there they'll send it to his mother in Florida. Too bad. A lot of us would like to pay tribute to that guy. He was probably the most underrated actor in the business, except of course for his physical qualities. Did you notice how that dog never once stole the scene from him? That's talent! Ask any actor. Yeah, I would have liked to go to the funeral. In fact, he once told me, once when he was in one of his morbid moods, he said, 'Michael, when I die I hope you'll be at graveside, chug-a-lug a can of beer, then toss the can in on the coffin and yell *Cut*.' "

"Wow," said Bimbo.

I then told him about the memorial party planned by Empie and Boris. Though it was primarily for Jerome and Doris, I surmised there would be no objections to celebrating Harold as well.

"Leave it to Boris," said Michael.

"You know him?"

"Sure. He worked on a couple of films with us. He didn't work out. But he said all he wanted was the experience, anyway. Called it an art piece. Kinda nice."

"He never mentioned that," I said.

"He's not ashamed of it," Michael insisted. "Not everyone can make it in this business. It's nothing to be ashamed of."

"Did he know Harold well?" I asked.

"Well, they worked together. In fact, that's how Harold met Jerry. Jerry was living with Boris and Empie at the time."

At this point, a curly-headed young man came bounding into the room. "Georgie," said Michael, "cool it. You'll upset the cops." The young man went pale, mumbled "excuse me" and left quickly.

"Who's that? asked James.

"Name's Georgie Porgie," said Michael. "A Unit. You can understand why anyone around here would be nervous about a known cop," he nodded to Bimbo. "But Georgie is nervous about anything."

"Georgie," I mused, trying to remember something.

"You know him?" asked Michael.

An unclear bell was ringing somewhere. "No," I said. "I don't believe I do."

We all said farewell and departed the establishment of Michael Bingham. As they were driving me back to the Y, and after James and Bimbo had made their reviews of the movie, James turned to me from the front seat.

"That party," he said, "are we invited?"

"Yes," I said without hesitation. "In fact, I think you should be there." I did not know why I said it at the time.

Chapter XVII

Caught up as I had been in the adventure of visiting the film studio, I forgot to worry about my physical condition. Now that I was returning to the Y, some of the previous feelings returned. I had never before known a hangover to hang over quite so long. If only I might be allowed to sleep.

"Boy, you sure don't know how to take a hint!" was O'Brien's post-mortem of our preceding scene together.

"It's all right," I tried to reassure him. "It was only a joke."

"You shoulda made them read something to you," he ignored me. "If they don't, it isn't legal." I nodded submissively as he handed me my key. "You look beat," he said. "Why don't you go get yourself a sauna, take a swim?"

"You mentioned someone Jerome Lamphere once submitted for membership here. Did you ever find the name?"

"Oh yeah," he said. "I finally looked it up last time I was over at the membership desk." He took his wallet from his hip pocket and removed a piece of paper. Instead of reading it, he set it down for me to see. "I'm not supposed to give out this information," he explained.

"Susan Denham" was written in O'Brien's awkward scrawl. Susan Denham. "Any address?" I asked.

"We didn't have a record of one," O'Brien shrugged.

"Well, thank you," I said, pocketing the paper. "If anything more turns up, I hope you will inform me."

"Will do," he said. "Now why don't you go have that sauna. It's on the sixth floor right off the pool."

"Perhaps I will," I said, and left for my room.

I could not get the name out of my mind. Susan Denham. Susie? Sue? Miss Denham? *Ms.* Denham?

Properly togged in swimming trunks, tennis shoes and my L Street Handball tee shirt, and in that waning-hangover dreamlike state during which it is unwise to cross streets and the like, I eventually found myself wandering in the athletic wing, but on the wrong floor. As I emerged from the stairwell, I was confronted with an oval track upon which several gym-suited men and a token number of girls were running. It circled around the upper third of the gymnasium where O'Toole and I had entered this building the night before. But now it was well lit, and the floor below was filled with more gym-suited beings participating in a calesthenics class. An out-of-sight, out-of-tune piano valiantly attempted to follow the variegated rhythms of the exercisers.

How sharply it brought back the memory of my own calesthenics classes, and Doris giving her all at the keyboard. How pleasant it had been, though tinged with sadness, to share her first occupation with her. Even her ill-concealed laughter at my attempts to keep up with the class ... even that laughter was ephemeral, seeming only to contrast with the sadness that replaced it.

It was as well for both of us that she finally had to find a position closer to her home, one that required more than a Monday through Thursday involvement. It gave us both nightmares.

In her nightmares, she was locked in at the athletic club with her own unposted mail, there to be forgotten throughout the long weekend until her creditors unlocked the door on Monday morning.

I had nightmares about being forever committed to the calesthenics class. Physical activity for its own sake seemed pointless, embarrassing and exhausting. I experienced a secret relief when Doris left the class, and I was able to depart it, turning greater attention to my beloved handball.

Refiling the memory in my brain, my attention was directed outward. I discovered that I had found my way from the gym to the pool.

A few men and a couple of bathing caps bathed in the chlorine water. Their goggles or squinting eyes were, perhaps, a convenient excuse to avoid conversation. The ladies were clearly ill-at-ease in this room whose very walls seemed to exude the former state of a male stronghold, and the men, no doubt thinking bitterly of the longlost days when they could swim here without the restrictions of bathing trunks, plowed reluctantly into the water.

At the back of the pool was a curtained window. Through a steamy parting in the curtains I could see a mop of hair resting against the pane. The sauna. I was just about to enter when a young man helpfully indicated that this was the women's sauna I was about to violate. Ours, he told me, was down a short aisle and further to the back. I thanked him, followed his directions, went into the proper sauna and sat there in the great heat, deceptive as Jamaican rum, which drains the daytime's poisons from your pores and many thoughts from your head.

For a short moment I again pondered the name Susan Denham. Was she an actress in a television soap opera? A name on a porno poster? I could not remember. What's in a name? Peter Piper. Mr. Bob. Chicken Coquette—now, there was a name! I smiled. Well, perhaps Susan Denham's name was no more real than any of the others.

Eventually, I emerged from the sauna, having steamed away the furrows in my brow. I hastily showered, now eager for bed.

As soon as I reached my room, the phone was ringing. It was Martha.

"Are you all right?" she asked. "Will you make it to Boris and Empie's tonight?"

"I'm just very tired," I said. "I know it's shamefully early, but the last couple of days, you know . . ." I trailed off into momentary subconsciousness. Indeed, sleep had not come easily in this city. The humidity alone would have made it difficult, but in addition I had managed to spend my first night in a police station and most of my second playing handball and drinking. This was my third night.

I was aware that some parts of life were going on exactly as planned. Martha would be spending this Monday evening with Boris and Empie. Nearly all the people in this city would go on, totally unaffected by the incidents of the past few days. But Jerome would not be arriving back in New York today. Doris would not be meeting O'Toole as planned. And there would be no Harold on a stage of a theatre in the combat zone of Boston. The thoughts whirled about the room.

"Have you been up all day?" It was Martha.

"Yes," I said with feigned alertness.

"Tell me about it tomorrow," she said. "Lunch?"

"Fine," I said. "I'll meet you at your office."

"Can I pick the place?" she asked.

"Yes," I said, "anything. Please offer my apologies to Boris and Empie."

"Don't worry about it," she said. "Go to sleep." And she hung up.

I had barely replaced the receiver when the phone rang again. "Martin," said O'Brien, "I've got a feeling you'd rather not be disturbed this evening. That so?"

"Can you arrange it?" I asked.

"Righto!" he said cheerfully and hung up.

I contemplated leaving the receiver off the hook, decided that would not be necessary with O'Brien looking after my best interests, and I had barely gotten into bed when there was a knock at the door. It was O'Toole.

"Martin?" he asked. "Are you sleeping?"

"Not yet," I said as I opened the door.

"Ah, but you're about to. Good idea. You look beat, if the truth were known.

"Yes," I said. "I am rather tired."

"I won't disturb you then."

"I'm rather tired," I repeated.

"Well, it can wait," he said seductively.

"Until I have regained my sanity."

"Sleep, me boyo, that's what you need," he said. "How about breakfast then?"

"Breakfast, yes."

"I'll wake you about eight or nine. That okay?"

"What time is it now?"

"Only seven-thirty or so," he said glancing at his watch.

"Then eight or nine should be just about perfect."

"Goodnight then."

"Goodnight," I said and closed the door. As he walked away I could hear him singing the silly tune we had made up the previous evening.

Fare thee well, my lady.
Farewell, my own true love...

The faintly discordant sounds blended and evaporated into the distance of the hallway outside as I returned to bed. Ah, poor James! A spirit that wants to sing and a voice unable. Long and painful study has proven, to my satisfaction at least, that my beloved Irish (like the American Indian) are an unmusical race. John McCormack, that greatest of artists, was a freak of nature.

Then, suddenly, there he was, John McCormack, standing on a stage, embraced by the curve of a grand piano, and singing,

... Until they hang me highdee,
You'll be my turtle duhhhhhhhhhhh...

and his voice ascended high, high into that ethereal region he knew so well but which the rest of us could only experience through him.

He repeated the short song, but the piano behind him became discordant, and I ran around to see who dared spoil my song and McCormack's rendition of it.

There sat a man in a black suit, on a swivel piano stool, and he was pounding the keyboard with his fists. I asked him to stop.

"What's wrong?" he asked in a voice which seemed familiar. "Bach used most of the same notes."

"Yes," I spluttered, "but the way you're putting them *together* doesn't make sense. There's no meaning to all those notes jumbled up together that way."

Stopping abruptly, his discords echoing in the cavernous concert hall, he swiveled on his stool and faced me. It was Jerome. "Well," he said, winking at me, "as soon as I get rid of all the notes that don't belong, it will be just as good as Bach!" He got up and started toward the darkened wings of the stage.

"Wait!" I called after him. "Come back!"

"I'll be back," he called over his shoulder as he continued on his way.

McCormack had stopped singing. "Are you standing on my stage?" he demanded.

"Yes," I admitted, once again in awe of him.

"Then what's your stage name?" he asked. "Michael?"

I could not speak.

"Georgie?" he asked, his voice rising in impatience.

"I don't have a stage name," I finally admitted.

"Then get off the stage!"

I sat bolt upright, suddenly wide awake. Susan Denham! Susan Denham! For a moment I almost seemed to remember, but it flew by as quickly as it came, before I could grasp it.

I let my head drop back on my pillow and instantly returned to slumber. I only remember that the rest of the night was filled with fitful dreaming. But, on the morrow, whatever answers might have been given me in sleep were gone.

Chapter XVIII

"Well, me boyo, I must say you're looking better than I've seen you in recent days," James said after I'd opened my door.

"Yes," I said, fully dressed and waiting for him, "and I'm ravenous."

"Nevermore," he grinned, and we proceeded to breakfast.

He said nothing more until I had consumed some coffee and several forksful of eggs and bacon. I hardly noticed his admirable silence until the hunger pangs had subsided. It was not until then that I realized I had eaten nothing on the previous day. In fact, owing to circumstances, I had taken very little nourishment since arriving in New York. Not since that Thursday evening with Dr. Sterne—and even that dinner's excellence was clouded by its perfection—had I enjoyed food so much as at this moment. Gradually, I slowed to my customary bird-like pace. It was not until then that James spoke. "Would you now be ready to digest some information?" he asked.

"Fire away," I said.

"Yesterday, while you slept," he said, "Bimbo and me had a few drinks and went over all the details of the case. And we came to a few conclusions about the culprit we're after. Many details were very carefully considered, the position of the body on the bed and so forth, even the way the blood was splashed on the wall. There's a lot there that seems very deliberate." He paused.

"Go on."

"Bimbo and I are thinking that while the murderer was executing a carefully thought-out plan, something happened that wasn't anticipated, something he wasn't ready for, and that made him stupid. He had to suddenly improvise on the plan."

"What could have happened?"

"Well, look at it," he said. "It's planned to look like suicide, which it did, but when it's almost over and the killer is about to get away, maybe Dorie walks in the door. Suddenly, he has to improvise. He acts impulsively, clobbers Dorie, and then with two bodies lying around and you coming home at any minute, he has to make some quick decisions that don't come up to the quality of his careful planning. Okay, quick change of plans, because it probably won't look like suicide now. So make robbery the motive. He grabs one of the manuscripts. It was only an accident that it was the least valuable of the ones you own."

"Well, I countered, "it had to be someone who knew there was *some* value in the missing manuscript."

"I suppose so," he conceded. "But if he knew Jerry, he might have learned something of your small collection. He might have known *where* it was without knowing *what* it was."

"Then why didn't he just take them all?"

"He wasn't thinking logically!" James said, sounding a little piqued.

"Why did he tape it beneath my window?" I suppose I was testing him.

"A burglar's instinct. Not to be caught with it. Get it later, maybe, when the heat's off."

"What about the car?" I persisted quietly. "Why would a killer wash half a car?"

"To get rid of fingerprints. He probably didn't have the time he planned on to do the whole car." Seeing my skeptical expression, he countered, "What's more, we think that the killer lives right here in New York!" I raised an eyebrow. "Jerry had been living here. The gun came from here. And Peter Piper was killed here. It all points to this city. It had to be someone here."

"You are assuming that the same person murdered all three victims."

"Yes." He eyed me suspiciously.

"What does Doris have to do with New York?" I asked him. "Is *she* connected in any way with this city? Think!"

His stiffness crumbled for a moment. "No," he said. "She never mentioned this place."

"Are you *sure?*" I persisted.

He thought a moment, then his jaw set squarely out, as was his wont. "I'm *sure!*" he said.

I recalled something Holliman had said about O'Toole. *Was* he lacking in imagination? "The traditional methods," I told him, "are not the only methods, nor are they always the most productive." He seemed to bristle, his back getting stiffer. I tried then to put him at ease. "Well, I suppose a lot of what you say makes sense, about this being a New York case, I mean."

"So," he smiled cautiously, "that means you and I, my boyo, are in the right place at the right time. Sergeant Holliman can't solve this case in Boston. It's partly a New York case."

"Do you have a suspect?" I asked.

"Not yet," he said, then added "do you?"

I shook my head and finished my coffee. "Do we know where Harold Hauser was last Thursday night?"

"Piper? No. Where do you think he was?"

"I don't know," I admitted. "But I know who might. You remember O'Brien mentioning someone Jerome proposed for Y membership?"

"Have you found him?" he asked.

"No," I said. "But I know her name. It's Susan Denham."

"Well, we'll see if we can't track her down," said James, "ask her some questions." He made a note in his notebook.

After breakfast, James and I adjourned to my room and enjoyed a quiet smoke, the only kind I dare allow myself without feeling pains in my chest. James, as a matter of fact, was unnaturally quiet, lost as he must have been in his own private thoughts, and I was given an opportunity to indulge in mine.

If one were to take the fingerprints seriously—and perhaps for a moment one should—how could they be explained? It was difficult to believe that Doris shot Jerome, then was clouted—painful term—by Harold. It seemed somewhat more plausible that Harold did them both in.

But then who killed Harold? Was this a murder unrelated to the others? Could it have been a suicide based on remorse? Was there a New York accomplice who thought it wise to omit such a talkative individual?

"James?" I asked, breaking his revery. "What more, if anything, is being discovered about Harold's friends?"

"Well, we have met Michael Bingham, of course. I rather like the fellow and would hesitate to question him unnecessarily. Still and all, there may be more that could be done in that area, if you know what I mean."

"What do you mean?" I asked.

"Well, the gun was last seen in the studio."

"Yes," I said causing him to beam, "you're right. If it was not used after the making of *Bad Guy* then we know from the film that the only prints on it would have been Peter Piper's." His eyes went out of focus. "Chicken Coquette wore gloves."

"Yes," he said, "and we saw the gun wiped clean in the film, used by Piper, then replaced in a plastic bag."

"I would think that a careful investigation of Harold's friends would be in order," I suggested.

"Bimbo is checking out everybody in Hauser's address book."

"Among them might be that Susan Denham. Harold didn't strike me as someone who could keep a secret very well. So someone in the address book might know something. In fact, before he died, Harold seemed obsessed with telling me all he knew at our first opportunity."

A deadly silence suddenly filled the room. So wrapped up was I in my line of thought, I completely missed all signs of the approaching storm. James had been studying his shoes during our conversation. Now he looked up at me, very slowly.

"What else do you remember," he carefully measured his words, "about Harold Hauser?"

"He had two conversations while I was there," I said. "I don't think he mentioned the name of the first person he was talking to. Yes, he did." Suddenly my dream of the previous night was recalled. "Michael?" I remembered McCormack asking me. "It was Michael," I told James.

"Bingham?"

"I don't know for certain, but they did seem to be talking about a film this Michael was going to make. They were discussing someone named . . ." I hesitated. Again I recalled McCormack asking, "Georgie?" "Georgie, I think," I told James. "Yes, that was it. Georgie. I think Georgie had to be persuaded to work on a film." Now I remembered clearly. "It sounded as if Georgie was supposed to be in the film . . . something about a front shot, and Georgie being reluctant to do a front shot. Do you suppose that meant nudity?"

"Why did they want him especially?"

"I remember from the second call," I said. "Georgie was a sound man, but apparently he was going to be asked to double in brass."

"I see."

"The second call was from Georgie himself, it seems. And while this Georgie person was on the other end, Harold was explaining some things to me about Jerome, about the novel."

His eyes narrowed and smoldered. "What about the novel?" he asked.

"Oh, didn't I tell you?"

"No, you didn't tell me."

"Well, apparently Jerome was imagining his own murder. According to Harold, Jerome was utilizing characters from his life and surmising about their motives for killing him and about how they might get away with it."

"Well," said James through tight lips, "now that seems to put more meaning on the disappearance of the novel, does it not?"

"Yes."

"And do you think this Georgie person overheard what Harold was telling you?"

"*I* would have if I had been on the other end." I said. "In addition, Harold tried to arrange a meeting with me that evening, to 'talk about things' as he put it. Georgie could have heard that part very easily."

"I see," said James.

"I don't say that Georgie, whoever he is, had anything to do with the murder of Harold Hauser, but it may be worth looking into."

"That it might," said James.

"Because," I continued, "as Martha and I were leaving and Hauser started after us to assure himself that I would indeed return that evening, he told Georgie he'd call him back. So you see?"

"See what?" asked James.

"Well, this Georgie is, quite possibly, the last person to

talk to Harold Hauser before he died."

"B'jaisus!" he shouted abruptly, quite surprising me. "You are a veritable goldmine of information, are you not?!" He got up and moved furiously toward the door. "There was a Georgie at Michael's studio. Remember the curly-headed young man? Very nervous, he was. Georgie Porgie, as I recall. Right there in front of us. And nobody questioned him. Perhaps that would have been *too* traditional."

"I just thought of it," I protested.

"Well, think some more!" he snapped, turning from the door. "Think if maybe you don't know who the blinking murderer is, but it hasn't occurred to you to tell anybody about it yet." Then he recovered his composure somewhat. "I only mean, Martin, that it would have been convenient if Bimbo had known this before he started his investigation." Then, the anger rising again, he left, being deliberately careful not to slam the door behind him.

I sat there dazed in the aftermath of his abnormal frenzy. I had not recovered before he returned, partially opening the door and sticking his head into the room.

"Martin, me boyo," he said in his most gentle leprechaunish tones, "if you get any other memories like the last ones, would you be so kind as to let O'Brien at the desk down there know where we can reach you?" I stared up at him stupidly. He smiled back at me, "And whatever you've told me today, plus whatever else you have yet to remember, will you kindly, like the Blessed Virgin, ponder them in your heart, and don't go telling them to anyone else?" I nodded, and then he closed the door again.

I could hardly blame James for his anger. But there were so many details, and it wasn't always easy to know which were important. If only somehow Jerome could keep the promise of my dream and return in some way. If only he would make things even half as clear as the voice of John McCormack.

I tried, in my mind, to recapture that clarity. But all I could hear was someone drumming on a piano.

Chapter XIX

There was clarity—and precision—in the typing of Liza Merriweather.

Mr. Bob waved me into the office as he hung up the telephone. "Well, Martin, how do you find our wicked city?"

"Very nice," I mumbled.

Liza paused in his typing long enough to ask, "How many movies did Alice Faye make?"

"Leave it blank for now," said Mr. Bob, "and say hello to Mr. Webb. Where's your manners?"

"Hi," Liza grinned at me.

"Well done," said Mr. Bob, and Liza resumed typing. "Any new developments?" he asked me.

"Nothing to speak of," I said, remembering James' instructions. Mr. Bob raised his eyebrow as if waiting for elaboration. "Since I last saw you, we have been concentrating on Peter Piper," I said.

"Oh yes," said Mr. Bob. "I believe he was here once. I recall we made jokes about his not being famous enough to slander." Mr. Bob smiled, "He said he was working on it very hard and that when he was famous enough, there would be plenty to slander him about. I only met him once, but I liked him."

"Do you remember why he came here?" I asked.

"He came to get Jerry. They were going to the Y together."

At this moment, Martha came in. I bid adieu to Mr. Bob, reminded him of Boris and Empie's party which he said he was looking forward to, and I left with Martha.

"Are we dining in your usual place?" I asked, hoping to be taken to the scene of Jerome's last luncheon.

"No," she said, "that's just a greasy spoon. I have a better idea."

We got into my car and proceeded uptown. Her driving was not incompatible with the personality of the Grey Ghost, and I relaxed after several blocks.

"It won't be fancy," she said, "but it's my favorite place for lunch and a lot better than most places we could afford."

"Price is no object," I lied.

"It's my place," she laughed.

I had suspected as much. "Had I known," I said, "I would have brought something to contribute."

"No need," she said, pushing her hair back over her shoulder. "I'll just open some tuna fish and maybe slice up an avocado."

As I was pondering this, the car slowed on a pleasant one-way residential street on the upper west side. Once again, save an illegal and quite damp spot near an open hydrant, there seemed to be no parking spaces available. I found this quite predictable, of course, but she cursed the situation. I was about to instruct her in Sterne's Law when she pulled over and double parked. "The cops only come through during the tow-away hours," she reassured me.

We got out and entered the hallway where we paused as she opened her mailbox and extracted about four envelopes and a circular. "A letter from daddy!" she exclaimed. She opened same and read it to herself as we climbed the five flights to her apartment. She finished the letter as we arrived at her door. We were both puffing.

"It's much easier going down," she said as she breathlessly handed me her mail, found her keys and fumbled to match up various ones with various locks.

The door opened on a very small studio apartment. On the far end the ceiling sloped toward the window, giving it a quaint garret effect. There was a real brick fireplace at one end and a dirty white sofa at the other. A small closet of a kitchen was in one corner, and a somewhat larger bathroom was off the short hallway by the entrance. The apartment was painted white, and there was a clean white rug on the floor. The apartment had the air of one recently tidied in anticipation of a visitor.

"Just put that stuff down anywhere," she said as she preceded me inside and went immediately to a dresser. I followed her instructions, placing her mail on a trunk in front of her sofa. "Make yourself comfortable," she said, taking a man's shirt from the drawer and tying the arms around her waist. "Like my apron?" she asked.

"Very practical," I told her.

"It was Jerry's," she said, pinning her hair atop her head. "You want to look through his stuff while you're here?" She nodded toward the open drawer.

I looked inside and saw a pair of blue jeans, some socks, underwear and a few magazines. "Was there nothing else?"

"Just some bourbon." She nodded toward the kitchen. I raised my eyebrows. "Want some?" she asked.

"A little bourbon would be nice," I suggested as I sat.

"I didn't know anybody drank a *little* bourbon," she said. "Jerry always drank a lot. I'll fix you one like his... lots of water," she said, cramming a glass full of ice cubes, "and a little bourbon," filling it to the top. "You might as well drink it 'cause I don't." She handed me this horse-killing drink. I said, "Oh, my!" or something equally complimentary and began to sip cautiously. No sooner had I done so when I remembered Harold had died from drinking Jerome's bourbon.

"I like scotch," Martha said as I heard her pouring same. "I poured some bourbon last night, out of habit I guess, before I remembered there was nobody to drink it."

"So it went to waste," I murmured as I tried to find some deadly aftertaste.

"No," she said. "I drank it. But I didn't like it."

"This is very nice," I sipped with more relief than she understood, as she settled near me on the white rug next to the off-white sofa.

"It's a spider web," she explained, thinking I meant the apartment, "and all the flies are gone. This whole thing," she gestured to take in the room, "... all designed to lure Jerry away from his apartment. I made it as homey as I could, figuring he missed that quality since he left his wife. Even got this new rug to surprise him when he got back from Boston. Did everything I could to make him forget his guilt, and his apartment and his roommate and every other thing. Lot of good it did me!"

For a while, we consoled each other and drank. When my drink was half gone, she repaired to the kitchen. "I'll make lunch," she said. "I can hear you if you want to talk."

"Actually," I said, "if you don't mind, I'd be curious to look at those magazines in Jerome's drawer, if they are Borman publications."

She returned in the process of opening a package of rubber gloves. "Help me, will you?" she asked. "They're hard to put on when they're new." I helped her, and then she opened the drawer and removed the magazines. "Yes, they're ours alright," she said. "Help yourself. Jerry always used his own name, so you'll know which articles he wrote."

As she busied herself in the kitchen, I scanned Jerome's articles, hoping that a cursory appraisal would be revealing. But, alas, I only discovered what I already knew, that Jerome was very adaptable. I would imagine that he could write for the *Farmers' Almanac* and *Ladies' Home Journal* with equal conviction. "What's the most frustrating situation in the world?" he once asked me. "I don't know," I obliged him, "what *is* the most frustrating situation in the world?" And he grinned and answered, "Two chameleons meeting." Then he laughed, and a moment later, when I got it, I joined him.

When I remembered the years Jerome had played the teacher role, despite his unhappiness, and his being a husband to Doris despite the bad timing, and then to live with Harold, and then to write articles for fan magazines... when I put it all together, I realized why he thought his joke was so hilarious. Jerome was an expert chameleon, instinctively adjusting his colors to a variety of environments.

"Penny for your thoughts?" Martha came into the room carrying a cold collation: tuna fish salad, avocado slices, lettuce and some crackers. I was instantly ravenous and she had barely set it down on the coffee table-trunk before I tore into it voraciously. She enjoyed the scene for a moment and then, after asking my permission, once more returned her attention to her mail. "Bills!" she complained, and then: "What's this?"

"Hmm?" I asked, my mouth stuffed with food.

"It's from Boston," she said.

I swallowed quickly. "Open it," I said.

"It doesn't say who it's from," she said as she opened the

envelope. She removed a piece of paper which had apparently been ripped from a three-hole loose-leaf binder. "My god, Martin!"

"What?"

"The novel," she said. "It seems to be a page from Jerry's novel."

I reached for my bourbon, and instantly remembered my dream in which Jerome promised to return. Despite this psychic preparation, I was quite astonished, even to the point of rudeness. I was, in fact, about to get up and read the page over her shoulder, I blush to remember. But then I saw her face. It was as though she were reading a love letter from someone she had not seen for a long time and never expected to see again. It was a private moment upon which I dared not intrude.

When she had finished, she held the page out to me in a trembling hand. The following is a reasonable facsimile.

–10–

could have been the perpetrator or the victim. There was no accounting for taste. Yet one was usually held accountable.

She wondered as he picked the piece of glass from her toe if, after everything was settled, they would be lovers. And if so, for how long? After he had completed the operation, she stuck her foot in the stream. She watched a small trickle of blood flow out like a scarlet thread and become diluted, very much like love itself. Then the blood stopped as the wound was frozen shut by the icy, purifying water.

"He liked the woods." Her eyes trailed upward, and the sunlight filtered through the leaves and eyelashes. She closed her eyes.

"If you had murdered him...?"

"Yes. In the woods." She opened her eyes and looked directly into those of her inquisitor. "But we don't know that he's murdered. We don't know that he's dead." Her tone was pleading.

"We're pretty sure we'll find a body." He threw a pebble into the water and watched it sink into the bull's eye of its own ripples.

"You might find two."

He looked up, questioning. But she was not looking back.

"He was seeing another girl, I think. Sue Denham. If you can find Sue, you might find him. You might find him alive." She looked at him now, her eyes moist with grief and jealousy. "And if not, I don't know who killed him. It had to be someone who loved or hated him more or less than I do now." She dimly watched the watery ripples his pebble had made reach out to touch those made by her tears, falling softly now like summer rain. "I loved him too much or too little. And I have been saved from ever understanding the full height of my passion. I don't know if that's a salvation or a

When I finally looked up, she asked me, "What do you make of it?" She stared at me numbly.

Sensitive to her emotions, I began obliquely. "Well, it's Jerome's typewriter." I held the page out to her. "I know from some letters he wrote me. The typewriter occasionally stuck on w's, and it created that blurred letter you see there. Did the same typewriter address the envelope?"

"It looks that way."

Indeed it did. "What's the postmark?"

"Yesterday," she said, handing me the envelope.

"Then," I stated the obvious, "he obviously didn't mail it himself. It would seem that someone in Boston is trying to tell you something."

"Yes," she agreed, "but not much I don't know already. That character is me."

"Well," I prompted, "it would seem that, if the novel is based on real people, Jerome had been murdered by page ten, and you are, after the fact, in the woods with someone unidentified, perhaps a detective."

She nodded.

"It also seems to indicate," I continued in my best scholarly prose, "that as far as the author is concerned, you were in no way responsible for his death. Your motive for killing him had not yet blossomed, as it were."

"There's another thing," she scanned the page. "Here." And she read aloud, "'She wondered as he picked the piece of glass from her toe if, after everything was settled...' meaning, I suppose, the murder solved ...'... if, after everything was settled, they would be lovers.' Get it? This is another guy. Jerry hasn't been dead for more than ten pages, and already he's got me flirting with the idea of someone else."

"Coupled," I continued, taking the page from her and finding the next significant passage, "with this: 'She watched a small trickle of blood flow out like a scarlet thread and become diluted, very much like love itself.'"

"Right," she said, touching my arm. "He was plagued by the idea of infidelity. He wasn't faithful to his wife, so he didn't expect anyone else to be faithful to him."

"Or rather," I suggested, "his guilt prompted him to envision his own punishment."

"Do you think there will be other pages?" she asked.

I remembered Harold's statement about Jerome's

fascination with possible motives his friends might have for his murder, about the ways they might evade punishment.

"I can't be certain there will be other pages," I told her. "But if there are, we have to be on our toes, so to speak, or there might be one very important page we will never see."

"Which one is that?" she asked.

"The one received by the murderer," I told her.

Chapter XX

After Martha had deposited me at the steps of the Y and I was beginning to ascend, James came bursting through the doors.

"There you are," he said. "Let's go." We started walking west at a fast pace.

"Did you find Susan Denham?" I asked.

"No," he said. "No mention in Hauser's address book. There are nine Denhams in the Manhattan directory, and none of them check out. We found something else, though." He looked secretive.

"Where are we going?" I asked, not picking up his obvious cue.

"We're meeting Bimbo at Hauser's apartment."

As we walked toward our destination, he told me that Michael Bingham had confirmed the phone conversation with Harold Hauser on the day of the latter's death. Michael had also led them to the other party, the young man known as Georgie Porgie, who had an underground reputation for sound recording.

"So we paid a call upon this Mother Goose character, Bimbo and I," said James. "He admitted talking to Harold that evening. Said he couldn't believe it was suicide. And he had something even more interesting to show us. If you're very good," James slowed his pace, "I will remove something from my pocket," he patted the breast of his summer jacket. "It will be a piece of paper,"

142

he said mysteriously. "It will amaze and astound you, me boyo, amaze and astound you."

"And the piece of paper," I said, "will no doubt be a page from Jerome's unpublished and unfinished novel."

He was instantly crestfallen. "Who told you?"

"If you will forgive my recent crimes of omission," I bargained, "I will remove something from my pocket." I patted my breast pocket. "It will be a piece of paper. It will be page ten of the novel."

"Mine," he said with rising spirits, "is page twenty-four."

We paused in a small park between two streets. Together, we extracted our treasures and proferred them to each other.

Georgie Porgie's page was xeroxed, but the original had clearly been ripped from a three-ring loose-leaf binder. It read as follows.

–24–

doubt about it.

"No doubt about it...really." Jordon Gordon picked up his thought. "According to Billy, Billy Club, the man was a creature of habit. If he's dead, whoever killed him probably knew those habits." He absently made a noose with the window cord as Brad sat quietly watching, neither seeing nor not seeing. "The guy was a real anal compulsive. At least that was the impression I got the couple of times we met. You know what that means, anal compulsive? Having a fetish for cleanliness and order."

Brad nodded absently. "I was thinking about something else, about an article you wrote for

Audio Magazine, the one where you discussed a sound which could not be heard, but which could drive someone mad or even kill him."

Gordon's fingers moved more nervously in fashioning the noose. He glanced furtively toward the wall of equipment which contributed electronic music to the otherwise spare environment. "That was a theory. Just a *theory!*"

"But if it was more, sound would be a weapon that could never be found. A person who knew how to use it that way might get away with murder." He saw Gordon raise his eyebrow, the contour of it seeming to match the curve of the cord noose. "What's that you're doing?"

Gordon looked down to see the noose and tossed it from him like a shock. It batted forward and back several times against the window like an insistent june bug, then it came to rest, the streetlamp outside casting the noose's shadow across Gordon's face. Seeing this in the bureau mirror, Gordon moved further left on the studio couch. "Just playing." He looked hurt. "Why do you make me feel so guilty? I barely knew the man. He was there when we filmed some quickies in Billy's apartment, and I saw him go around later, cleaning up and muttering. That was as much as I knew him! Why aren't you out talking to his girlfriends? Why pick on me?"

"It was made on the same typewriter," I said, "and probably ripped from the same binder."

"Yes?" asked James.

"We might assume that this Jordon Gordon is Georgie Porgie alias somebody else. Billy Club might be Peter Piper alias Harold Hauser. This person, Brad, could be the unidentified man in Martha's page, perhaps a detective."

"Anything else?" he asked.

"Only that it looks like a bad xerox copy," I said.

"It *is* a xerox copy. The original was left at the station for fingerprinting and so forth."

"I'm sorry," I said, "about handling Martha's page. I didn't think of that."

"No matter."

"Were there any fingerprints on this?" I asked, returning the Georgie Porgie page to him.

"Other than the recipient's?" he asked. "Yes, there were. The usual. Jerry's, Dorie's and Harold Hauser's."

Chapter XXI

"This senior patrolman," Bimbo nodded respectfully toward a silver-haired and expressionless policeman, "is here to keep us honest."

He inserted a key into a mailbox labeled "HAUSER-LAMPHERE." It opened to reveal an assortment of mail. The inscrutable policeman reached inside and, with a white-gloved hand, gingerly removed the contents. The four of us then trooped up one flight to the Peter Piper memorial apartment.

The room had been black-dusted like my own apartment. There was evidence of a search.

"Gentlemen?" Bimbo gestured for us to join him as he sat on the rug.

While we struggled in vain to be comfortable on the floor, the uniformed policeman brought a small lamp from the desk, it being dark in the apartment, and he lit it for us. Then he placed the bundle of mail in front of us like a campfire for so many boy scouts. His gloved hand spread the mail out with the gentle touch of a harpist.

Amidst it all was clearly seen the envelope with the Boston postmark. It was addressed to Harold. Bimbo pointed it out, and the implacable policeman lifted it, carefully peeled off one end of the envelope, delicately reached inside and removed a paper which he unfolded and purposefully placed on the rug for us to read. We examined it without touching it. Like the others, it had evidently been torn from a binder.

–74–

"I put up with his habits, I suppose you'd say. I let him have his privacy as much as I could. I bought a separate bottle of bourbon and didn't complain if he ran out and helped himself to mine. And that usually happened when one of his girls was visiting."

Brad continued to look through the scrapbook. "That's interesting."

"What is?"

Brad's voice was casual. "The separate bottles idea. If *your* bottle was poisoned and he drank from it, it would be hard to prove you intended to murder him."

"I needed him!" The protest seemed sincere. "Without him, I couldn't have kept this apartment."

"I'm sure you could have managed." Brad closed the scrapbook and held it out to Billy. "All these parts you've played, you must have been paid for them."

Billy's eyes rolled upward as he held the scrapbook to his chest and settled back on the sofa. "You've got to look at the big picture." He became whimsical. "The brighter a star is, the sooner it can burn out... especially in my profession."

Brad smiled. "I know what you mean." He was as serious as possible.

"So he was part of my security, I suppose you might say. I didn't want to waste my money on any more rent than necessary."

"On what then?"

"Well, I collect things. Old things. I don't know if they're worth anything. Maybe they will be someday. Anyway, I enjoy having them around."

"Well..." I sighed.

"The collecting thing," James got up from the floor to stretch his legs and paced restlessly around the confines of the room, "that could tie in with Martin's music manuscript. It could mean that Harold was the one in Boston." He paced some more, then stopped and lectured us, "Put the three pages together, and it looks like our dear Jerry was keeping company with more than one girl."

I found that as difficult to believe as the thought that Jerome had been a marijuana smoker, but reminded myself that none of Jerome's friends, including me, knew everything about him. I casually glanced to the pipe rack. "By the way," I asked, "is it the pipe on the right that was used for marijuana?"

"It is," said James. "How did you know?"

"Because that pipe wasn't there three days ago. Then there were only five pipes in the rack."

James took out his notebook and made a note. "My compliments to your powers of observation," he said.

I again turned my attention to the novel page before me. "Perhaps," I suggested, "I should return to Boston to see if I have received some interesting mail."

"Maybe Dorie got something," said James.

"Yes, quite possibly."

"Well, nobody has to go back to find out. Let Holliman do it. It'll make him feel a part of things." James turned to Bimbo. "It would be helpful if we all had copies of this." Bimbo nodded and grinned.

"What else is there?" Bimbo looked at the other seven pieces of mail.

One piece seemed to be a personal letter to Harold, a brightly colored envelope addressed in a florid longhand with circles dotting the i's. There were four bills and two circulars. One circular was addressed to Jerome. The other was addressed to Susan Denham. *"Hello?"* said Bimbo with a counterfeit British accent.

"What did I tell you?" said James.

"What indeed?" Bimbo said with a grin which kept getting broader.

"What the devil are you smirking about?" James asked. "I can't see that you've had anything to offer."

"But I do," said Bimbo. "I do."

"Then where is it?" asked James.

"Right here," said Bimbo, nodding toward the gloved policeman who had already placed the mail in a celluloid folder and was now placing this in a manila envelope. "This senior policeman has one of the best minds on the force, and I'm sure that by now he has an opinion. Do you have an opinion, Mac?"

"Solve your own cases," Mac grunted.

"Mac wasn't always a patrolman," said Bimbo. "He was once a detective, weren't you, Mac? But he got caught with his hand in the cookie jar, didn't you, Mac?"

"____ scapegoat," said Mac.

"Just give us your opinion," said Bimbo. "Is that too much to ask? And maybe, if you have a good opinion, you can be a detective again someday."

"I wouldn't help a crippled old lady cross the street," said Mac.

"He's a little shy today," Bimbo explained to us.

"____," Mac said.

"But I think he's getting used to us," said Bimbo. And

then there was a long, expectant silence.

"____," Mac said again, and went on. "____," once more, and again "____."

The finest mind on the police force seemed to me to be overly preoccupied with a single idea. But I soon learned that this was Mac's way of priming himself.

"You want to know what I think about this case?" he asked finally. "I think it's a lot of ____!" He paused for effect, looking around at us with disdain. "You kids haven't figured it out yet, have you? The guy who wrote this ____," he referred to the novel page, "he killed himself." He paused a long moment, a pause so long it demanded to be filled.

"Suicide?" asked James.

"You ask to be killed, and even if somebody else does it, it's some kind of suicide, I figure. Look!" Mac leveled his gloved finger in our direction and held it there for a long moment. "I've been on the force a long, long time. When I was a rookie, this guy," a thumb jerked irreverently toward Bimbo, "wasn't out of diapers yet. So I've done it all, and I've seen it all. And I can tell you there are all kinds of nuts in this world, and somebody asking to be killed... well, this ain't the first time, not by a long shot, it ain't. Wives browbeat their husbands when they're carving the meat... they're asking for it. Fruits sashay through a construction job yellin' anti-American stuff... they're asking for it. A whitey gets drunk and puts on a monkey suit to go to Harlem and look for the Cotton Club... he's asking for it. And a guy writes a book telling everybody how they can kill him, just in case they haven't thought about it...? Well, what do you kids think?"

"He's asking for it?" asked Bimbo innocently.

"Shove it," said Mac.

After a moment, I asked as gently as I could, "Do you

know who did it?"

He turned to me, and his expression changed. Now he became more kindly in his patronism. "Like I say, as far as I'm concerned, this guy killed himself. It doesn't matter who shot the gun. You could make a case for this Peter Piper porno freak killing the writer and his wife, and then Piper gets sorry later and kills himself. Now, that's clean. That way you don't go off looking for some poor slob who never would've thought of it if he wasn't taught who he wanted to kill, why he wanted to kill him, and for all we know, how to do it without being hanged."

"What about the pages that were mailed?" I asked.

"Piper could've arranged that when he was in Boston."

"But the postmarks..."

"People have been known to leave addressed, stamped mail with a friend for mailing later. Lots of ways."

"Fingerprints?" Bimbo asked.

"Who's gonna check out the prints on every postal clerk between here and Boston?" Mac countered. "All I'm saying is you kids should close this thing as quick and as painless as possible... without getting anyone else involved. If you got something against crime and want to be heroes, I hear there are a lot of rapists and muggers hurting people who want to be left alone. Why go after someone who only honored a murder request?"

We considered the wisdom of Mac's remarks, then the silence was broken by a sigh from Bimbo. "You've been very helpful as usual," he told Mac. "Well, let's get on with it. You can take that stuff back to the station. I'll be along in a minute, and we'll get in touch with Boston."

Mac grunted, took his manila envelope and started toward the door. On some impulse, I accompanied him. He opened the door and strode out, then looked back somewhat arrogantly. Not receiving any challenge from me, he smiled slightly. "I retire in two more years," he said. I nodded. He nodded back and then went about his business.

After I closed the door, I wandered back down the hallway to the bathroom. Desiring to splash some water on my perspiring face, I went inside and closed the door behind me. The bathroom, like the living room, showed evidence of a search. The medicine cabinet was open and nearly empty of bottles. Some band-aids had fallen out into the sink. A rubber glove had fallen away from its mate on the windowsill. I found it strangely depressing. How thin the walls were! I could clearly hear James and Bimbo talking in the living room.

"Okay," said James, "what was that all about?"

"Mac," explained Bimbo, "is notorious. It's why he was kept on the force after the scandal. He says a lot of gibberish, and sometimes it's hard to sort the nuts out of the leaves, but he usually sees something or other clearer than anyone else, or maybe he points you in a right direction."

"Well," said James, "they're teaching these days that a murdered person, without meaning to, many times plays a part in his own death."

"If you can believe psychology," said Bimbo.

"I'm only telling you what they're teaching." O'Toole sounded offended.

I returned to the living room hoping to be a buffer to James' sensitive spot, but I had no sooner entered the room when Bimbo raised his finger to his lips to caution us to be silent. Then he switched off the lamp. In a moment, we heard footsteps. It sounded as though someone were tiptoeing up to the door. We heard a key turn in the lock and someone come down the long hallway. The intruder froze in the doorway as he saw our shadowy figures. Bimbo aimed the lamp toward the doorway and switched it on.

"Georgie Porgie!" said Bimbo. "What an unexpected pleasure!"

Chapter XXII

It was indeed the curly-headed young man we had seen briefly at Michael Bingham's studio. If he seemed frightened then, now he was in shock. He neither moved nor spoke for what seemed a full minute.

"Come in!" Bimbo urged him. "Nothing to be afraid of." His offhand manner at least confused the young man if it did not put him totally at ease. "I don't think you've met Martin Webb. Martin, this is the young man who was so helpful to us earlier today." I offered my hand, and he took it limply. "And you remember Officer O'Toole. We were just leaving. Was there something here you wanted? It's all up for grabs."

"No," Georgie managed to say finally. "No. Nothing."

"You must have come for something."

"I thought I left something here, but I didn't. I just remembered I didn't." Having recovered his senses, he now avoided our gaze and kept finding excuses to put his hands in front of his face.

"When we interviewed you earlier today," Bimbo persisted, "I don't think you mentioned having a key to this apartment."

"Harold gave it to me."

"Why would he do that?"

Georgie was silent. His eyes darted about their sockets as though seeking a reasonable response.

"I think this guy's stalling," said James in an unnaturally rough voice. "Let's take him in."

"I don't think we have to do that," said Bimbo.

"You mean we can beat it out of him?" O'Toole's play-acting now became painfully obvious to everyone, everyone except poor Georgie who was too wrapped up in his own emotions to notice.

"Why don't you go get us some coffee," was Bimbo's wise suggestion. O'Toole took the hint, added a touch of insincere profanity and departed, slamming the door in an unnecessary touch to his performance.

"My partner," Bimbo told Georgie in gentle tones, "he can get a bit excited. Sometimes it's hard to control him. It's no wonder my profession has a reputation for brutality with cops like that. Did he ever hurt you before?"

"No," said Georgie. "I didn't meet him until today, and he didn't seem anything like this then."

"It's that Irish temperament," sighed Bimbo, "very unpredictable. One minute they're patting you on the back, the next..." he smacked the palm of one hand with the fist of the other. It made Georgie jump. "Well now, let's relax until he gets back. And whatever you forgot to tell us before, this is a good chance to get it out if you want to." With this, Bimbo lay back on the floor and waited. Georgie looked at me.

"I think it best," I told him, "for all concerned."

"I came to get some dope," said Georgie. "I mean if Harold left any lying around, I thought somebody ought to take it away."

"Do you know where he kept it?" asked Bimbo staring at the ceiling.

"He told me he kept it inside that sofa. He gave me the key and said I could help myself anytime I wanted. But I never did because it would be bad for me. But now that he's dead, I thought I'd get rid of it."

Bimbo got up and searched the sofa by reaching between the seat pillows and up the hollow back. "Weren't you here smoking dope recently?" he asked.

"No, I never did."

"That's too bad. I thought you might've been here last Thursday. You know, when those two people were killed in Boston. I thought then we wouldn't have to worry about *you* being in Boston. Get me?"

"I was here last Thursday," said Georgie. "I was here then with Harold."

"Smoking dope."

"No."

"What then?"

Georgie paused. "We were making a movie."

"Which I believe was the type of thing alluded to in your novel page," said Bimbo. He pulled a small plastic bag of a catnip-like tobacco substance from its hiding place. "You were right," he said. "But you really shouldn't get involved with this stuff before they legalize it." He placed the package casually aside. "Now tell us, why didn't you tell the police you were here Thursday night? Don't you see, it would have made our life a lot simpler, and maybe yours, too?"

"I'm sorry."

"But you didn't answer my question."

"What question?"

"Why you didn't tell us before." Bimbo was being patient.

"It's illegal, I guess," said Georgie.

"In what capacity were you working on this film?"

"I was doing sound."

"Interesting. That was also suggested in your novel

page. It makes you wonder how much of that fiction is real, doesn't it? Did you ever write an article about sound?"

"Yeah, one or two."

"One about a sound that could kill? Is that possible?"

"It might be. I don't know."

"You don't?"

"Sound can do a lot of things people don't realize."

"Did you ever think it could kill somebody?"

"I don't think so. I never wrote an article about it."

"Where would Jerry get an idea like that?"

"I don't know. I had this idea for a movie about sound being used to, uh, you know, turn people on. It was going to be an X-rated spy movie. Maybe Harold told Jerry about it. Maybe that's what gave him the idea."

"Oh," said Bimbo, "so you write, too."

"Well, I get an idea once in a while."

"Did you write the movie you were filming last Thursday?"

"No."

"Were you serving in any other capacity last Thursday?"

He hesitated. "I was in it, sort of. Just a small part."

"Do you usually appear in these films?"

"Not so you'd notice."

"What does that mean?"

"I wear a lot of makeup, moustaches, beards, things to disguise myself."

"Are you ashamed of your profession?"

"Well, my relatives back in Indiana, they might be."

"Do they go to films of this kind?"

"No, of course not. But, you know, people hear things."

"Was this the reason Harold never told us what he was doing that night?"

Georgie was beginning to perspire. "Harold had an agreement to work just for Michael."

"Did you often make your own movies in this apartment?"

"We used to, until Jerry got mad about the disruption."

"Which is also in the novel page."

"Yeah, but I never thought sound could kill somebody. He made that up."

"Why do you suppose you were in the novel?"

"I don't know. I hardly knew Jerry."

"You must have made an impression on him."

"I guess so."

"I suppose, like everyone else, you saw the novel beforehand."

"I knew about it."

"How did you know?"

"That same page I got, Harold read that to me once over the phone."

Bimbo was silent. The silence grew uncomfortable, and Georgie felt compelled to fill it. "So last Thursday we were just taking advantage of Jerry being away, and we were using the apartment again."

"I wonder why Harold didn't tell that to the police."

"As a matter of fact, he was worried about it. A couple of days later, he was talking to me about it on the phone. He wanted my opinion. Should he tell where he was that night? Would it look suspicious if he didn't and the police found out he'd given the gun to Jerry?"

"*He* gave the gun to Jerry?"

"That's what he told me."

Bimbo looked to me, then quickly back to Georgie. "How many people were here Thursday night?"

"Just me and Harold."

"Can you make a movie with two guys?"

"That's right. There was a girl, too."

"Sue Denham?"

"Not her."

"She wasn't in the movie?"

"Was she supposed to be?"

"Where can we contact her?"

"I don't know. I never met her."

"But you seem acquainted."

"I just heard about her. A couple of times when I talked to Jerry, I think he mentioned this friend of his, one he wanted to write music for us. But he never brought her around, or anything, not when I was here."

"Who was the girl?"

"I think he called her Susan Denham."

"No, I mean the girl who was in the film with you."

"I'm not sure."

"That seems unlikely."

"Okay. I know this'll sound like a lie, but it's the truth. I was working as an actor. Harold needed two guys and a girl."

"Then there were *four* people here that night?"

"Yeah, four. I was one of the guys. But I told Harold I didn't want to know who else was involved, and I didn't want them to know me. I'm sorry. That's the way I am. So I wore a disguise—moustache, beard, dark glasses, the whole bit—and I kept my eyes closed the whole time. There was another guy and a girl. But I don't know who they were. If you can find the film, then you'll know. But I can't help you there."

I had never heard such an implausible story, but Bimbo seemed to accept it. "I don't suppose you'd know where the film was?" he asked.

"No idea," said Georgie.

"Now, you said you talked to Harold on the phone.

That was the night he died?"

"Yeah, I guess so."

"And then you came over here for a short while. What sort of mood was he in when you left him?"

"I didn't say I came over here. I just talked to him on the phone. I didn't see him since last Thursday."

"Thank you, Georgie," Bimbo said abruptly. "I hope we can feel free to contact you if there are any more questions."

"Sure. Anytime. You know where I am. Can I go now?"

"Certainly." Bimbo held up the plastic bag. "You understand why I can't let you have this."

"Sure. So I lose. No problem." He started to go.

"Oh, one other thing," said Bimbo. "Where *were* you Saturday night if you weren't here?"

"I was out."

"Out where? Drinking?"

"I don't drink. I just wandered around, saw a movie."

"What movie?"

"A double feature at the Elgin. *Ninotchka* and *Anna Karenina*. I love Garbo."

"Anyone see you? Anyone you know?"

"I don't think so. That all?"

"Sure," Bimbo waved.

Georgie left.

"Interesting young man," I said when he was gone.

"Very interesting," said Bimbo as he resumed his search inside the sofa back. In a moment he removed what looked like a film can. "You know," he said casually passing the can from one hand to the other, "Georgie Porgie is also a very bad liar. He isn't even very good at telling the truth."

Chapter XXIII

Boris and Empie lived on a school street which was blocked to traffic, but not to patrol cars such as Bimbo was driving. The children swarmed around it, making loud noises, some of which they had no business understanding. The three of us sat in the car as the small faces peered in at us. Bimbo and James raised their windows, "so as not to dirty the interior of the car," Bimbo explained, "should the little darlings decide to throw peanuts."

James turned to me. "Are you sure you don't want us along?" he asked.

"No," I assured him, "that won't be necessary, and it might be easier without bringing strangers."

He nodded. "All right then, me boyo. We've other fish to fry. Talk to you later." I nodded and let myself out the back door. The children were like taffy that clung to and stretched from moving bodies, such as the car as it crept away, such as myself as I ascended the front steps and rang the doorbell labeled "Boris-Empie."

"Oh, hi there," said Boris as he opened the door. "Hi, kids," he said over my shoulder.

"I'm sorry if I'm disturbing you," I apologized, "unannounced in this way, but I actually did happen to be in the neighborhood."

"Uh-huh. I see," said Boris. "Well, please come in."

I did, and the children started to follow. Boris knelt

offers and suffered another long pause.

I decided to try Bimbo's offhand manner of interrogation. "Do you happen to have a snapshot of Susan Denham?"

Boris sat quite still for a moment, staring blankly, and then a smile appeared. "Yes, I believe I do." He went to the hallway where I could see him rummaging through a pigeon-hole cupboard, shuffling through papers until he returned with a snapshot.

It was another one of Jerome, but unlike my own candid of him and Doris, this one was poorly framed. He was shown standing before his apartment building, his left arm cut off by the amateur photographer. There was no one else in the picture. I looked questioningly at Boris, and he turned the snapshot around. There on the back in Jerome's hand was scrawled, "Me and Sue Denham."

"But," I protested, "there is no one else in the picture, only Jerome."

Boris smiled. "So it seems." He smiled some more. "Maybe she's outside the frame and he's holding her hand. Maybe she's taking the picture."

"Well, did you ever meet her or see her?"

"Not in person," said Boris. "Just that snapshot."

How would Bimbo handle a situation like this? I did not know, so there was another lengthy pause. "There's been a lot of excitement since I last saw you," I said finally.

"Beautiful."

"Jerome's roommate..." I ventured tentatively.

"Yes," he smiled.

"Harold Hauser."

"Yes."

"Uh..." I dug deeply for words. "Some of his friends would like to come to the...funeral...party."

"The more the merrier," Boris smiled, then became instantly serious and rushed back to the pigeon-hole cupboard in the hallway. He soon returned with a newspaper clipping. The article, which Boris held out to me, told of an incident when Peter Piper had been arrested by FBI agents who came pounding on his door while he was sleeping. It was headlined:

PORNO STAR SURPRISED IN BED!

And under the headline was a picture of Peter Piper himself, grinning broadly behind the large, empty glasses frames.

I smiled and nodded. Boris did the same, then placed the clipping on the table next to the snapshot of Jerome and Doris.

"You knew him?" I asked. "You knew Harold?"

"We made a movie together," said Boris. "Such fun. Real art."

"The movie was art?"

"*Making* it was art. Art is experience. That's why I did it... as an art piece."

That much established, it now became easier for me to get to the point of my visit. "Have you received anything unusual in today's mail?" I asked.

"What do you mean, unusual?" he asked, and paused. "Perhaps if you explained what was usual, I could tell you if we received anything unusual."

I explained about the pages of the missing novel and asked if he had received one. His eyes seemed to disappear into his forehead for a moment, and then they refocused on me. "Yes," he said, "I believe we did." With that, he returned to the pigeon-holed cupboard in the hallway, and in a moment he smilingly brought me an envelope with a Boston postmark. "I thought it was a fine work," he said, "but I didn't connect it with anything or anyone. I just liked it. But now that you mention the novel, I guess this could be that." He removed the page from its envelope, unfolded it and handed it to me. It had all the characteristics of the others.

–52–

Barnie was talking now. "I suppose it was beautiful. Trusting strangers with your secrets, that's beautiful, isn't it, Jacques?"

"Uhuh. Beautiful." Jacques folded his legs into each other and swayed gently in the cane-chair swing suspended from the ceiling. "More than beautiful."

"More than beautiful." The echo was Barnie's. She hunched forward toward Brad, staring inside him to see if any part of him could possibly understand. "That's why I think he's dead. He'd been thinking about dying. He even asked us to kill him." She rested back against the bolster of the sofa, watching Brad for some expression, waiting patiently.

Brad looked up from the picture of the girl he had never seen before. "That's difficult to believe."

Barnie smiled. "It wasn't a *direct* request. He asked us how we might kill him and not be blamed. I told him we'd do it as an art piece. I would tell him to crawl into a sack and tie it closed from the inside. But I wouldn't touch him, nor the sack. I would merely tell him to do something and he would do it. And I wouldn't know what Jacques was going to do."

Jacques spoke dreamily as his chair swung back and forth in the sunlight. "Without knowing he was in the sack, I would stage an art piece of my own. I'd have several of my students stab the sack with knives. It would be beautiful. A perfect crime."

"Except for one thing." Brad rushed to Jacques and abruptly halted the swinging chair. "How would you dispose of the body?"

"Don't you get it?" Barnie was suddenly behind him. "We wouldn't have to."

"No," said Jacques, "because it would have been an accident."

"Do you have any idea what this means?" I asked Boris.
"Mean?" he asked back. "Does it have to mean something?"

Chapter XXIV

"I've been trying to reach you," Martha told me as I entered the Borman Publishing office.

"More pages?"

"Mr. Bob got one in the afternoon mail. Have there been others?"

"Five so far, including yours."

"I didn't get one," Liza pouted and pretended to wipe a tear from his eye, then brightened and asked, "Who?"

"Susan Hayward," Martha snapped and turned anxiously to me, running her hand lightly over the tight lines of her upswept hair.

"What movie?" asked Liza.

"Please, Liza!" said Martha, then to me: "He left it here for you in case you came when he was out."

"*I'll Cry Tomorrow*," prompted Liza.

Ignoring Liza, Martha took a page from Mr. Bob's desk and handed it to me. This one had not been punched for a three-ring binder, nor had it been torn from one. I sat at Jerome's old desk and read it.

–81–

Mister blinked, then turned to the clerk. "Lunchtime."

"Right, Chief." The clerk quickly left.

Mister looked at Brad and smiled. "Jealousy. I'll

be candid with you. Not jealous about his love life; that's too complicated. Something else. I come into this office five days a week, more when there's an emergency. I make a good living, but it takes a great deal of time and effort, and it also takes a certain suspension of one's integrity, standards and aspirations. Then along comes ____ who uses me. He just turns out a living's worth of pages, with very little personal sacrifice, and he allows me to support him in doing the things I always thought I would be doing someday. I hated him. You might as well know. Someone else would tell you eventually." Mister held his gaze on Brad for a moment, then slumped away from his desk and stared out the window. "Are you sure he's dead?"

"Are you?"

Mister opened a magazine and showed it to Brad. The article was written by ____, and it was about a famous singer and his Mafia connections. "The last time someone wrote like this about this guy, he wound up dead. What can I tell you?"

Brad sat on the edge of the desk and looked down at Mister. "You could tell me who told ____ to write the article."

A short page, or an unfinished one. I had no sooner finished when the phone rang. It was James. "Meet us at headquarters, Police Plaza, communications," he told me. "Holliman's calling there in half an hour. He particularly wanted you to be there. He practically said he'd have my badge if you weren't."

I assured James I would be present, hung up, and explained to Martha that I had to be going.

"First tell me," she pleaded, "what about Mr. Bob's page?"

"It's very close to what Mr. Bob told me that he told Jerome last Thursday, except for the Mafia article. Did Jerome ever write one like that?"

"No, never." She took the page from me. "Can you guess what this blank space is for? Here where it says 'then along comes blank.'"

"That shows up elsewhere," I said. "My guess is that Jerome hadn't decided on a proper pseudonym for himself."

"Like he already didn't exist," suggested Martha.

"Yes," I said. "Something like that." I took the page with me and left.

Chapter XXV

I was glad I was not returning to the same police station in which I had spent Saturday's sleepless night, for that was, in my imagination, something like Purgatory, a place which like a bus or train station was a non-place between places. The Communications Center was a beehive of activity and a welcome contrast. Encompassed by the sound of teletypes, I felt a quickening anticipation that the drama was about to resolve itself and that my appearance in this new setting was somehow an important part of the denouement.

I was directed to a particular location where I found James, Bimbo, a teletype operator and a teletype machine. Bimbo was seated at a small table and talking on a telephone. James pulled over a chair for me and introduced me to the teletype operator whose name was Steve, a man of few words who merely nodded.

"You're just in time for some funny afterthoughts from the dimwits in the lab," Bimbo told me as he replaced the receiver. "They're pretty good at afterthoughts."

"Now what?" James asked him.

"Nothing too important," said Bimbo. "They just got around to telling us that the envelopes and pages weren't typed by the same person. The envelopes have a more even touch." He tapped his fingers on the table, four-four time, and tried unsuccessfully to laugh. "Oh well, at least the fingerprint analyses make sense."

"How's that?" I asked.

"Martha Simms' page has the same three set of fingerprints: Jerome Lamphere's, Doris Lamphere's and Harold Hauser's plus two unidentified prints, presumably Martha Simms' herself and those of present company," he nodded to me. "Harold Hauser's page," he went on, "thanks to careful police handling, contains only three sets, the usuals. The envelopes are all messed up with prints. It's the heavy perspiration in this hot weather we've been having, that's why we've got more prints than we know what to do with. It certainly defies the best analysis by the summer help in our lab. I just hope they're capable of developing that roll of movie film."

I hesitated to intrude very aggressively on the somewhat electric atmosphere, but did presume to show them the two new pages from Boris and Mr. Bob. Before anyone could comment, the telephone rang. Bimbo lifted the receiver to his ear. "Put it through," he said. Then he cradled the receiver atop a plastic receptacle.

"Hello?" Holliman's voice was heard emanating from a small speaker.

"Hello, Sergeant," said James. "We're all here, me, officer Schwartz and Mr. Webb."

"Alright," said Holliman. "We found pages at both locations. At your apartment, Webb, and at the home of Mrs. Lamphere. The pages and the envelopes have apparently been typed by different people on the same typewriter." Bimbo smiled. Holliman continued, "Our laboratory discovered some dyed cotton lint on Lamphere's clothes and also under Mrs. Lamphere's fingernails, but it doesn't match anything else in Webb's apartment."

"What does that mean?" I asked.

"Can't be sure. Could be something Lamphere was wrapped in. Whatever it was, Mrs. Lamphere had her hands on it. I have another piece of information for you. According to the Wessex post office, Mrs. Lamphere phoned them early Thursday morning and requested that her mail be held there and delivered on Saturday. That probably means she expected to be away from her home Thursday, the day of the murders, and at least part of Friday." He paused to let this sink in. "Her Volkswagen is still missing. Write this down." He gave us the license number of the car. "What have you found out?" he asked with the tone that expected a tangible response.

James explained about the recent pages that had been uncovered. He said he'd send them back on the teletype.

"Yes," said Holliman, "do that. But I think I should tell you that I no longer consider this strictly a Boston case." We exchanged glances. "There are too many details associated with where you are," he said. "In fact, if you ignore the fact that the blood seemed fresh on Lamphere's face, then the coroner's report suggests that he could have been murdered in New York and transported to Boston, although Mrs. Lamphere was probably disposed of here. At least half of this, and maybe more, could be a New York case."

"That makes sense," James said hesitantly, "but there was no blood in the car, was there?"

"No," said Holliman as Bimbo picked up the rhythm of his table tapping. "Webb, what do you think?"

"It's worth considering," I said cautiously.

"Yes," said Holliman, "we must consider all things. What would you say if I told you I took the liberty of interviewing some of your friends and associates?"

"I would expect you to do so," I said. "After all, I was at the scenes of crimes."

"Your Miss Pinkham..." (Dear Miss Pinkham, what a thrill it must have been for her to be interviewed by the police! What an opportunity for her to exhibit her knowledge of procedures!) "Your Miss Pinkham," he continued, "has suggested that if anyone was likely to come up with the answer, it was you." James and Bimbo laughed good naturedly, as though Holliman had been telling a joke. "In fact," said Holliman, "you have excellent credentials as a musical sleuth. Let's see what you make of deathless prose. We're going to try to reproduce it as best we can on this machine, and we'll follow up with xerox copies later. Both of them have apparently been torn from a three-ring binder. Both of them have the prints of Mr. and Mrs. Lamphere and Harold Hauser. Okay, here comes the first one, the one addressed to Mrs. Lamphere." And the machine to the best of its ability, reproduced the page from over 200 miles away.

–18–

"I sat here alone all day. I have no alibi. Should I be afraid to tell you that? I mean, will that be the mistake that sends me to the gallows? Because I have a feeling they're going to blame me for this. If I wasn't so schizoid, I'd help them do it, because the truth is I don't care. It would be an easy way out." She glanced furtively at him, too timid to hold the look, and then away, back to the piano upon which she started to play Rachmaninoff's Second Symphony. It was sad.

"I had motive, anyway." The melancholy music seemed to underscore what she was saying. "I might as well tell you. It'll come out, anyway. He wanted a divorce. I'm not the type to fight a thing like that, but I will procrastinate. And I know he's worth more to me as my dead husband than as my ex-. So that's the motive, money. Money and...the fact that he was always able to find someone else to love and I wasn't. The woman scorned, you know, like which Hell hath no comparable fury."

Brad sat there a moment, quietly, as the music played. Then he walked over and touched her shoulders. "*Always* find someone else?"

"The last girl he was seen with wasn't the one he left me for." The music continued for a moment, then without a pause in the playing, she said, "I wish you wouldn't touch me." Brad removed his hands. "Nothing personal, you understand. It's just that I've inspired so much short-lived pity, I'd rather not inspire anything at all, not for a long time."

He sat on the bench beside her. "Will you help me find the murderer?"

The music stopped. "No. I want nothing more to do with ____, not to avenge his departure, not to examine his life. I just want to forget now that he ever existed."

"Come through alright?" Holliman's voice shouted before we had time to fully digest the contents of the page. We assured him that we had it. "Okay," he said, "here's *your* mail, Mr. Webb." The machine promptly picked up the cue and printed the following:

–27–

This man was the most unusual person Brad had ever met in all his years on the police force. This

man had been unusual for even longer than that.
"G. Robin Spine!" Brad shouted. "Stop reading!"

Spine looked up from the book. "If you wish. But there is something here that might prove useful one day."

Brad removed his shoes and began to dig at Spine's wallpaper with the toenail of his left foot, his right foot searching casually for tufts in the threadbare carpet. "Go on," he said with divided enthusiasm.

Spine cleared his throat, then read:

"Otello, my true love know. There she is,
Unnoticed, Sue of Denham. Hamlet, she's
Like April's pseudo donuts, nymphet for All
my moist dreams. But, come, you too relate.

"Go on," said Brad, picking some loose plaster from his left toenail, as his right continued its fearless journey into the tractless waste.

"That is all."

"What is it supposed to mean?"

"Exactly what it says, give or take a syllable," responded Spine.

"Tap the feet;
Just keep the beat."

Brad's toe found a piece of napping or something of the sort and pulled it up for examination. "This is not carpet," he said.

"No, to say otherwise would be spineless. It is a piece of fuzz from the brain of Jerome Lamphere. A late night, no doubt. Drinking, no doubt. Then coming to this fatal page, obviously too drunk to deal with G. Robin Spine, or whoever that might represent. Too dead drunk. But with the iron grasp of rigormortis, he bellows his way, however senselessly, to the prescribed bottom of the planned page at the end of the protracted daily quota. If he lives, he rewrites. No matter. Life is a rewrite. Only death can be new. Tis a consummation, *cherchez la femme,* etc. hahahahahahah

"Well?" Holliman asked.

"He may have been intoxicated when he wrote it," I suggested, "as he was when he wrote me a letter or two."

"Is it a private joke?"

"There are the Shakespearean references to Othello and Hamlet, and we enjoyed paraphrasing Shakespeare, playing with the verse and so forth. So it's personal to that extent."

"Is that a typo on Othello?"

"No, that's the name of the opera version."

"Anything else?"

"Yes, the 'Sue of Denham' reference," whereupon I related all we knew about that lady of mystery."

"So what's he saying with *'cherchez la femme'*? Find Sue Denham?"

"It's possible."

"What about the end, the 'If he lives' business?" asked Holliman. "Was he anticipating his own death?"

"Entirely possible, either at his hand or someone else's," and I told him what I knew about the novel.

"Gentlemen," Holliman widened his focus to all of us, "can you name me one particular thing about this case which is odder than anything else?"

"There's so much," James said, "it would be mighty difficult to pick one thing that was odder than anything else."

"You, Webb?"

"Well," I said cautiously, "my friend James has perhaps put his finger on it."

"What are you saying?" asked James.

"That there is, as you said, so much," I smiled at him, as Bimbo tapped his fingers thoughtfully on the table. "I mean," I continued, "there is an excellent rhythm that Bimbo is tapping out. But compare..." and I pounded the table rapidly with my knuckles in rapid counterpoint to Bimbo. "We're doing the same thing," I explained, "except I'm doing *more*. If you remove what doesn't belong, I'm doing the same drumbeat as Bimbo."

"Kitten on the keys," Bimbo smiled, and I recalled my dream in which Jerome pounded a piano with closed hands and then explained it would be Bach when all the wrong notes were eliminated.

"Yes, in a way...a random selection," I said. "But eliminate what doesn't belong, and it is a clear, simple rhythm or tune."

"Spell it out!" snapped Holliman.

I had forgotten Boston, but now reminded, I moved close to the speaker. "Sergeant," I said, "forgive the obtuseness of my remarks. But you will recall our conversation about the importance of determining what is missing, or what should be there but is not."

"Yes."

"The other side of that coin, of course, is what is there that should not be. And one of the oddest things about this case is, as James suggested, that there are too many clues. Therefore, they may not all fit. Therefore, eliminate the extraneous or the misleading, and it will be perfectly clear. You yourself suggested this."

"I did?" asked the voice over the speaker.

"Yes," I said, "when you said that if we *ignored* the fresh blood on Jerome's face, he might have been murdered in New York. And once you ignore that one fact, then many things point to New York as the scene of the crime. But you have to *ignore* the fresh blood. You might say that solving this case is a matter of hearing the symphony hidden amongst the notes a child pounds on a piano."

"How can you ignore fresh blood?" asked James. "This isn't a symphony!"

"Let the man talk!" bellowed Holliman.

"Forgive the musical allusion," I said, "but it expresses it best. It occurs to me now that we may have been concentrating so hard on the wrong notes that we have been distracted from solving the case."

"It isn't new," said Holliman. "It's just a different way of saying that some clues are not clues. But can you be more specific where the case is concerned?"

"No," I admitted, "not yet. It only just came to mind, and I'm blathering to some extent. But I think I'm beginning to hear the melody."

"Can you whistle it?"

"No," I smiled. "Not yet. But perhaps soon."

Holliman was silent for a moment. James and Bimbo stared at me. "Anything else?" asked Holliman.

"Not that comes to mind," I said.

"Would you like copies of the other pages now?" Bimbo came in quickly.

"Send them on," said Holliman. "And Webb?"

"Yes, Sergeant?"

"Can you solve the case?"

"Yes sir," I spouted before I quite realized what I was saying. "I think so."

"How soon?"

I was committed and plunged ahead. "A couple of days, I think."

"Then do so," said Holliman. "Don't kill anyone, and don't say I told you to, but *solve* it! And, O'Toole...?"

"Yes sir?"

"If you want to put on a uniform again, cooperate with the librarian, and never breathe a word if he screws up."

James made a helpless gesture to Bimbo.

"Sergeant Holliman," asked Bimbo, "are you asking policemen to cooperate with a civilian rather than the other way around?"

There was a pause at the other end, and the sound of breathing. "I realize I have no control over you, Schwartz," Holliman said finally, "but I hope you'll go along with it."

"My superiors have already asked me to cooperate with you and Officer O'Toole, and if you ask me to cooperate with *Mr.* Webb, I will certainly do so. But . . ."

"Yes?" asked Holliman as though preparing the answer to a question not yet asked.

"But," continued Bimbo, "my cooperation might be better directed if I knew the reason for your . . . well, would it be fair to call it an 'unorthodox' request?"

"Is this call being monitored?" asked Holliman.

"No sir. Steve is here, that's all."

"Who's Steve?"

"The teletype operator."

"Is Steve a talker?"

"Are you a talker?" Bimbo asked Steve.

Steve shook his head no.

"He's not talking," Bimbo told Holliman, and Holliman chuckled on the other end. We all laughed then, except for Steve, and somewhat nervously.

"All right," said Holliman and paused. Then his voice began haltingly, carefully choosing the words. "Mr. Webb . . . has established himself in scholarly circles . . . as a superior . . . detective, having a knack for . . . uncovering answers . . . to questions . . . that baffle his colleagues."

"That would be in the field of music," suggested Bimbo.

"Yes," said Holliman, "but his solutions to many musical puzzles are solutions any of us might have come up with if we possessed his alleged talent for deduction. They are not necessarily based on specialized knowledge, but on a superior intuition, according to the people I've talked to." I could feel the blood rising to my temples.

"In other words," said Holliman, "he may be some sort of genius. Now, I don't know, of course, and neither do you. But I'm ready to take a chance on him. And the reason I'm ready is that there's been a mobilization of South Boston, a massive demonstration on the Commons this morning. The people of Southie are making very loud noises that the culprit be found and that Southie streets be once more safe for God-fearing citizens. Nothing quite like it since busing. Well, this might be easy to ignore, except the mayor quieted the demonstration by promising action, and then he got the police chief to promise action. It finally came down to me . . . and I had to promise *results*. Now, you put Webb's reputation next to my job being on the line, and maybe you'll understand this 'unorthodox' order of mine."

A long silence, then "Yes sir," said Bimbo. "I understand. We'll cooperate with Mr. Webb."

"Okay," said Holliman. "I'm waiting for the pages."

There was a click of 'goodbye' at the Boston end. The air was settling uncertainly about me as Bimbo picked at a sliver of the table and James watched Steve transmit the pages.

"If I have somehow violated some code of ethics, I apologize," I told them.

James cleared his throat. "Ah, that's all right," he said.

"You have become involved," said Bimbo, continuing to pick at the table, "in a certain situation. You see before you two men who are dedicated to crime-solving and who consider themselves professionals in this respect. Now, I'll tell you a secret about professionals of all kinds. Most of them feel that everyone else is more professional than they are, that they are holding onto their undeserved status through some phenomenal stroke of luck. They live with the fear that they'll be unmasked someday, and it'll be all over. Now, when a superior places an amateur above the professional, then the amateur—in this case, you—is that which proves the professional's deep-seated, worst thoughts about himself. And the amateur is not, by any means, a sight for sore eyes."

"Nonsense!" yelled James, telling me that Bimbo had stated the truth.

"Gentlemen," I said, "I am sorry for any hurt feelings, and I hope they are momentary, for I am no policeman, and I don't know procedures. I will need you in this!"

"Well," said James quietly, "I expect you will."

"I'm intrigued," said Bimbo, "about this discordant symphony idea of yours. Do you think you can sort out the false notes?"

"Perhaps," I said. "At any rate, I've only given myself two days."

"Thursday," said Bimbo.

"Boris and Empie's party," mused James.

"If everything goes as well as I think it will," I said, "it will be then—exactly one week after the first murders—that we might hear the symphony."

"I guess all the music will be there," Bimbo grinned.

"And, hopefully," I said, "all the instruments as well."

Chapter XXVI

All the necessary facts have now been presented; it only remains to put them together in the right way—to eliminate some false notes, rearrange others, and perhaps add a few that have not been heard but which are obvious mathematical necessities in the composition. It is tempting to merely reveal the solution.

However, my editor assures me that we cannot abandon the narrative at this point, but must plunge on and illustrate *how* the answers were arrived at and the circumstances under which they were revealed. She (the editor) feels that such things are obligatory. I oblige with deference to her publishing experience, but with a small apology to those scholars who may be reading this for educational purposes and who are now impatient for conclusions.

Overburdened with Holliman's faith, I began to leave police headquarters. I say "began" because James and Bimbo were now intrigued with the bizarre situation and had, it seemed, endless lists of advice and cautions. They supplied me with copies of all the novel pages and of all the notes they'd taken. They offered to check in with me at intervals. It was an outgoing, effusive and totally uncomfortable situation for all of us. The moment required fussing, anything to give them purpose.

I told them they had worked hard, looked tired, needed

rest and so forth. I asked that I would always be able to reach one of them, pointing out that this was a rare moment in the annals of crime, a moment when an amateur was given official permission to hang himself, and I would doubtless need them to cut me down. But what else could we do for the moment? We shook our heads helplessly from side to side, resigned to the next 48 hours.

By the time I finally worked my way out the door, they were feeling quite sorry for me, and in the early hours of stagefright, I was feeling sorry for myself.

It was about 8:00 P.M. on Tuesday night when I returned to my room at the Y. I did not emerge for almost 48 hours. While in this retreat, I was sustained by one hot (and later, cold) pastrami sandwich, one piece of cheesecake (one of the nicer things about New York), one apple, and one fifth of Irish whiskey. A duplicate of the latter had been given to O'Brien to protect my privacy during these crucial hours.

From time to time, I could hear James walking noisily outside my door, clearing his throat, singing that same silly song so that I would know it was he and might, perhaps, invite him in to participate in the solution. I did not (forgive me, James), and after a while, so intense did my concentration become, I was aware of nothing but the case.

I began with some food and some whiskey. Then I moved a small table away from the window and placed a chair by it facing the wall. Upon the table I placed a glass of whiskey, paper and a ball-point pen. Now I was ready for Part One of what I have come to call "my system," the assessment and reassessment of the facts until I would fall unconscious on the bed and the answers would, I hoped, crystalize in a dream.

We will not deal with *all* the mental gyrations which I forced upon myself in those hours before sleep. Suffice it to say that the unravelling was a complicated process and, while working on an intellectual level, I traversed many blind alleys and many mazes that finally brought me back to the starting point.

I began by getting my notes in order. I made a list of the novel pages in the order they were written.

Page	Subject
10	Martha
18	Doris
24	Georgie
27	Me
52	Empie & Boris
74	Harold
81	Mr. Bob

Then I put the pages aside. Next, I jotted down the names of everyone with whom there had been contact, directly or indirectly, since the previous Thursday evening. I crossed out names, put them back, crossed them out again. The reader will understand my thoroughness by the names that were finally eliminated as suspects;

> Dr. Sterne
> Miss Pinkham
> Sarah O'Toole
> O'Brien
> Sergeant Holliman
> Bimbo Schwartz
> Mac

I suppose a mystery fan would be quick to suspect a distinguished Harvard professor, a stereotyped maiden librarian or a YMCA desk clerk, not to mention any of three policemen, especially after Empie was quoted saying they make the best murderers. If your suspicions have moved in any of the above directions, you too have been swayed by extraneous notes.

Turn your attention now to the other list and its notations compiled from my own thoughts and from James and Bimbo's notes. The first two are understandably brief.

> JEROME LAMPHERE— May have poisoned his own bourbon, thereby killing Harold.
> DORIS LAMPHERE— May have shot her husband before she herself was killed.

Beyond these, I not only indicated the reason each name was on the list, but also, where appropriate, two alibis, (1) for Jerome and Doris' murders, and (2) for Harold's.

> HAROLD HAUSER— (Peter Piper) Georgie says Harold took gun (for Jerome?) Had burglary record. Would be most likely to know technique of hiding stolen property near scene of crime. Would have greatest opportunity to plant poison in bourbon. (1) Making movie in New York, according to Georgie. (2) Suicide?
> MARTHA SIMMS— Was intimate with

Jerome and showed dislike for both Doris and Harold. Regarding the "stolen" music manuscript, she is a musician of some kind. (1) At home alone, there to receive call from police about 1:30 Friday morning. (2) With me.

JAMES O'TOOLE— Was intimate with Doris and had access to my apartment. (1) Not included in notes, but likely he'd been seen at Fenway Park and that Holliman checked it out. (2) Unknown.

EMPIE & BORIS— Empie showed anger over Jerome's having wasted a part of Martha's life. It was her idea to "celebrate" the deaths. She justifies the murders by saying that the victims never really lived, anyway. Both of them justified many things as art pieces. (1) Claim to be with each other. (2) With me.

MR. BOB— His jealousy of Jerome
(Andrew Roberts) seemed real enough.
(1) Working late at office with Liza. (2) Home with family.

LIZA MERRIWEATHER—On and off the list several times. Appears only because his position at Borman might be elevated through assuming some of Jerome's responsibilities. (1) Same as Mr. Bob. (2) All-night movie. Confirmed by date.

MICHAEL BINGHAM— Access to the gun. (1) Making movie with several others. (2) Same.

CHICKEN COQUETTE—Access to gun. "Intimate" with Harold. (1-2) Same as Michael.

GEORGIE PORGIE— Access to gun. Access to Harold's apartment. Nervous. Why did Bimbo suspect he was lying? About what? (1) Making movie with Harold, unconfirmed. (2) Seeing movie alone, unconfirmed.

H. MARTIN WEBB— Of course, I knew I did not commit any of the murders, but I was

SUSAN DENHAM— included in the police notes, so there's my name for good measure. (1) With Dr. Sterne, indisputably confirmed. (2) With Martha, Empie and Boris, confirmed. Included for obvious reasons. It seemed odd that she had not yet come forward and that the only two people who could help me find her, Jerome and Harold, were dead. (1-2) Unknown.

It was now about 5:00 A.M. Wednesday morning. After a shower, I returned to my room, finished the pastrami sandwich, and poured myself another whiskey. I stared at my list, sensing that there was something very obvious that I wasn't seeing. No matter. I was certain to see it later. Now I began another kind of list, the sequence of events as accurately as I was able to reconstruct from memory and from police notes.

Thursday— 4:15 P.M. — Jerome seen driving away from NYC in a dirty auto.

6:00 — Coroner suggests earliest time of Jerome's death.

	10:00	— Approximate time of Doris' death.
		— Mrs. Donahue sees a man who is perhaps carrying something into my house.
	10:20	— Man emerges, walks off carrying, perhaps, a green plastic bag.
	11:00	— Bodies discovered.
	11:30	— O'Toole discovers house is empty.
	12:30	— Discovery that auto is half clean.
Friday—		No events of note.
Saturday—	6:30 P.M.	— Probable time of Harold's death.
	9:00	— Body discovered.
Sunday—		— No events of note.
Monday—	? A.M.	— Novel pages postmarked in Boston
Tuesday—	? P.M.	— Pages arrive in NYC.

Just as the meaning in my list of names eluded me, so did the meaning in this list of events. However, it did serve to get some facts in order.

It was now 9:00 A.M. Wednesday morning, but that was all I noticed. I suppose there were traffic sounds outside. I suppose it was once more oppressively hot. But I can't be certain. I was preoccupied with the next task. Another list.

What We Do Not Know

> Who killed anybody.
> Why anybody killed anybody.
> Where Doris was going when she left Wessex.
> The location of Doris' Volkswagen.
> The location of most of the novel.
> Why the least valuable music manuscript was taken.
> Why no one has mentioned hearing a gunshot.
> Why the blood on Jerome's forehead was moister than it should have been.
> The identity of the man seen entering my house.
> The whereabouts of Susan Denham.
> Who mailed the novel pages, and why.
> Who typed the envelopes.
> Why the only fingerprints are those of the deceased.
> How and why the BMW was half cleaned.

When this was finally organized in the above order, it was mid-day. I ate an apple and finished the whiskey in my glass. Then I spread out the four lists before me looking for connections among them. But they blurred before my eyes. For a moment, I even hallucinated the three faces of the deceased floating upon my neatly ordered pages like images on projection screens. This was my first indication that I was exhausted and that it was time for part two of my "system."

I fell onto the bed and into one of the most complicated, yet intensely clear, dreams I ever remember experiencing. I found myself moving through space on a cloud like a white magic carpet. The planets and stars were rushing past me at incredible speeds, accelerating until everything became a blur. I heard someone pounding on a piano behind me and discovered I was not sitting on a cloud, after all, but on a grand piano, and Jerome, as in the previous dream, was pounding its keys. He looked up at me and winked, then slowly unfolded his fists until his fingers touched the keys. Now he played music, Elizabethan I think, and the blur around me slowed and formed into images.

Doris was playing a second piano in the Boston athletic club where she once worked. A gymful of men were participating in a calesthenics class.

"Monday morning," called Doris. "Mail truck's here," and all the "males" ran out of the room. "Hope they take it all," said Doris, "especially my bill payments." This made me recall her previous technique of staving off creditors. Before I could remind her of this, she fell off the piano stool, bleeding and apparently dead.

"Get some plastic down," shouted Mac as he came stomping into the room. "Don't mess up the floor and you can get away with murder. The way you do it, that's what counts." Then he shouted, "Count!" his command echoing in the empty gymnasium.

All counterparts of the novel characters were racing on the running track which encircled the room halfway up.

"Page ten," called Martha as she ran by.

"Eighteen," said Doris, miraculously revived.

"Twenty-four," said Georgie.

Mac nudged me. "Twenty-seven," I said.

"Fifty-two," said Empie and Boris in unison as they ran side by side.

"Seventy-four," Harold called as he ran by, the only one who looked at all as though he belonged on a running track.

Mr. Bob gave emphasis to my impression by bringing up the rear in a floral gymsuit and pronouncing, "Eighty-one."

Now the characters had assembled in a line on the gym floor. "Reverse count," shouted Mac.

Mr. Bob stepped forward and held out a magazine. "The last time someone wrote like this about this guy," he said, "he wound up dead. What can I tell you?"

"If *my* bottle was poisoned and Jerry drank from it," said Harold, "it'd be hard to prove I intended to murder him."

I realized they were all quoting from their novel pages.

"Without knowing he was in the sack," said Boris as Empie nodded her agreement, "I would stage an art piece of my own. I'd have several of my students stab the sack with knives. It would be beautiful. A perfect crime."

"Cherchez la femme," I said as they all looked at me.

"Sound would be a weapon that could never be found," said Georgie. "A person who knew how to use it might get away with murder."

"Might get away with murder," Mac broke in.

"Are you still coming here after work Monday?" Empie asked Martha.

"We were going to spend Monday night together," James whispered into my ear, "after she left work."

"You know," said Harold coming toward me, "I've got to go up there tomorrow night for a day or two."

The scene suddenly shifted to Boston's combat zone. Again I saw the marquee which proclaimed:

"IN PERSON—SUNDAY & MONDAY ONLY—
PETER PIPER."

Then I was inside the theatre where Jerome played honky-tonk piano in the orchestra pit. A spotlight lit up an easel upon which a placard announced "PETER PIPER," then the spotlight moved about the dark, empty stage as though searching for the famous porno star. But the search was fruitless, and soon Chicken Coquette appeared, scantily clad perhaps, but in *my* dream you can be certain she had some clothes on. She minced to the easel and changed the placard. The new one promised, "IF YOU KNEW SUSIE!" Jerome began to play this ditty as the novel counterparts came on stage and recited as follows:

MARTHA: He was seeing another girl, I think. Sue Denham. If you can find Sue...
DORIS: The last girl he was seen with wasn't the one he left me for.
GEORGIE: Why aren't you out talking to his girlfriends?
ME: (Being prompted) *Cherchez la femme!*
EMPIE & BORIS: (Together) Brad looked up from the picture of the girl he had never seen before.
HAROLD: He usually helped himself to my

	bourbon when one of his girls was visiting.
MR. BOB:	Not jealous about his love life. That's too complicated.

All the characters disappeared, and the piano resumed playing Elizabethan music.

A Shakespearean jester appeared, balanced on one foot and placed the other in his mouth. "There you go," said Jerome from the pit as he played, "putting a foot in your mouth again."

The clown let his foot drop to the floor and began to do a tap dance. "Tap the feet, just keep the beat," he sang as he tapped out the beat of the song which followed...

Otello, my true love know. There she is,
Unnoticed, Sue of Denham. Ham...

He broke off to kibitz with Jerome. "Sue of Denham?" He asked. "Was that the lady I saw you with last night?"

And Jerome sang,

Fare thee well, my lady.
Farewell, my own true love...

and then he told the clown, "That was no lady. That was my life."

"Life," said Harold as he appeared talking on the telephone and flipping through a loose-leaf manuscript. "We take our lives into our own hands every day we go out on the street in this city." He picked up the gun, placed it in a plastic bag and passed the bag to Jerome. Jerome vamped with one hand as a rubber glove reached up and took the sack from his other hand.

The gloves removed the gun and shot it at Jerome. For

a moment, the gun seemed to be a tailpipe backfiring. The music stopped.

The gloves lay now at Harold's bathroom windowsill, one finger pointing toward two bourbon bottles on the facing kitchen windowsill. A toilet flushed, and the bourbon drained from one of the bottles.

Martha, Mr. Bob and Liza were at the window, but it had become a different window. I came up behind them and looked down to the street where a BMW was driving off. However, its sound was not that of an automobile, rather one of human retching.

"Liver sauteed in chocolate," I said.

The retching sound increased in volume until overpowered by another, something like a hissing snake, or the fizz of a seltzer drink.

"I made a special tea for him," said Empie as she placed a teapot atop an open fire hydrant.

"The guy was a real anal compulsive," Georgie quoted from his novel page.

The retching sound seemed to explode from a tailpipe and blood was spattered on the Picasso mural of "Guernica." The blood fell down the painting like exclamation points to white flowers below. Then atop the flowers were scattered clear plastic bags, one of which held Jerome's head.

"Beautiful," I heard Boris say, as the mural was sprayed with water from the hydrant, washing away the paint as well as the blood, changing the mural into a wool-like white fabric which rolled off its frame and around the debris beneath.

On the wall where it had been hanging, I saw my own bedroom wallpaper streaked with blood. The off-white fabric and its contents moved sideways out of my field of vision.

As it did so, I saw the BMW being towed by the Boston police. Another tow truck came by with Doris' car, a loudspeaker at the top blaring, "NO PARKING THIS SIDE—TUESDAY AND FRIDAY."

A yellow Boston taxi drove by, lifted into the air and flew to answer a ringing telepone in the distance.

Then I saw that the off-white fabric and its contents were being eaten by a garbage truck, its digestive sounds providing the transition to reality.

I awoke to the tune of a real garbage truck in the real street below, that determined but lonely sound. I lay there wide-eyed for a moment, afraid that movement might blur some of the dream's details. I reviewed them all quite carefully. Yes, it was all there. Every visual and aural moment was there as clearly as though I were dreaming it again.

I arose and went to the table where the pieces of paper, my lists, still stared at me. I searched through other papers to find my own novel page. I reread it. Yes, now I understood.

I telephoned James' room. He had been waiting by the phone. "I almost broke in on your seance," he said impatiently. "Guess who was in that film Harold was making."

"Just bring it to the party," I said, "and a projector." I told him where I thought Doris' car could be found and requested that he establish a number of other points, all of which he took careful note.

"That's a tall order," he said. "Bimbo and I'll split it up, but I can't promise we'll be able to find out everything in time for the party. Better get started anyway. See you there."

Not time before the party? Ah yes. It was now 1:00 on

Thursday afternoon. I had actually been asleep for about 24 hours. Asleep? Or a grand awakening?

I returned to the table and my list of names. I picked up the pencil and circled one of the names. Then I circled another.

Chapter XXVII

It was not a symphony; it was a concerto. With all the sounds and notes in their proper order, a single instrument emerged dominant, supported by others. The melody was very sad. Or I was saddened by it, for nothing could dispel the melancholy which enveloped me as I walked to the party. The evening was as warm and pleasant as that of a week ago. That and the children laughing and jumping through the spray from an open fire hydrant provided ironic contrasts to my mood.

The contrasts continued inside the house. Pen-and-ink portraits of Jerome, Doris and Harold floated in the air, suspended from white balloons upon which had been painted angels' wings. Festoons and streamers of white crepe paper completed the decor. "White is the Oriental funeral color," Empie told me.

Also scattered about in random locations were an infinite variety of Oriental foods, international drinks ... and what may have been marijuana cigarettes.

As nearly as I could tell at the time, there were not more than ten people in a space a little larger than a handball court, among them Empie, Michael and a few members of the B Unit, Chicken, Martha and Georgie who drank apple juice. But the room seemed crowded because there were so many balloons and so many floating portraits of the dear departed.

Bimbo appeared without James. Michael promptly donned his familiar fatalistic expression. Chicken Coquette was, on the other hand, delighted to see her old friend, and she executed a back-breaking leap. Apparently accustomed to such exuberance, Bimbo withstood the charge.

"Do we have a suspect?" I asked him at my first opportunity.

"Shall we look at the house?" he answered. "Some of these converted brownstones are very nice."

Some balloons drifted before us as we ascended the stairs. We moved the portraits of the dead from us like cobwebs. Real and familiar faces appeared amidst the confusion. Boris had been touring the house with Mr. Bob and Liza. We briefly exchanged greetings as we passed on the stairs.

On the top floor Bimbo and I discovered the empty studio, and we sat on two chairs painted blue with clouds near a large canvas on which the multicolored word "word" was painted over and over in a small, feminine hand. The arrangement of colors, like colored dots in the Sunday comics, seemed in the process of becoming a portrait of William Shakespeare.

"So far," Bimbo grinned his approval, "you check out one hundred percent." He proceeded to tell me Doris' car had been found, that prior to its arrival at this place, it had been parked near the suspect's home, and that neighbors had heard backfiring. He told me about long distance calls made from the suspect's telephone, and about a delivery that a large, local retailer had made to the suspect's home on Friday. Finally, he told me about the owner of the sixth pipe in Jerome's pipe rack. "So it looks like the suspect is turning into the perpetrator," he said. "Of course, that's only the New York end and only half the story. Jimmy's working on Boston, and he might not be able to get all the answers tonight."

I told him what I thought James would discover. He seemed satisfied with my analysis, but not with my suggestion that the murderer be revealed at the party. He felt it more important that we build the case than take a chance on a premature revelation of what we knew.

"That would be a logical approach," I admitted, "and one with which my friend James would concur."

Bimbo smiled tolerantly. "There are good reasons for most procedures," he said. "Jimmy is a good cop."

"I know."

"It's only that inside him is a better cop wanting to get out."

"Yes," I said. "But the reason I'm glad he's not here now is it would have been difficult to convince him to dispense with procedures."

"I think I can convince him as another cop," said Bimbo, "if you can convince me."

After I had done so, he said, "Okay, leave Jimmy to me." He thumped me on the shoulder. "If he gets here with even half the stuff you think, we'll continue to 'cooperate.'" He grimaced comically over the distasteful word, then laughed. He picked up a handy easel. It recalled to mind the stage easel upon which Chicken placed placards in my dream. "And a sketch pad," said Bimbo as he found a rather large one. "You'll probably be wanting these." We returned downstairs.

As the party continued and grew in gaiety, as balloons burst and glasses broke, I often found myself less a participant and more a curious observer. With an alert and finely tuned social instinct, Mr. Bob sensed my apartness and descended on me.

"You know," he said, "if *this* were a part of the missing

novel, it would be the scene in which the murderer was unmasked."

"It is difficult," I said somewhat sadly, "to know the face beneath the mask."

"Difficult," he topped me, "and impossible. It has been said, you know, that if two people enter a room, there are really six people present: each person as he sees himself, each as seen by the other, and each as he really is."

"And what we know best," I said, "is how we see others."

"Would it be right on this occasion," he asked, looking at the balloons, "to consider how Jerry, Dorie and Harold saw *themselves?* I wonder about Dorie because I didn't know her at all. How did Harold see himself; as a sex symbol? And Jerome; an object of violence?"

"Why do you say that?"

"It's my understanding he envisioned himself the victim in his novel."

"It's possible."

"There you are. In fact, I wonder why there should be a witch hunt. Why even *look* for the murderer?"

A balloon was brushed aside, and there was Martha. "As nearly as I can tell, all three of them were unhappy," she said. "Maybe Jerry was asking to die, but in such a way that he wouldn't be responsible. I guess Dorie held onto his memory out of some apathetic need. Considering his sickness, that's not saying too much for her frame of mind, and she was probably as self-destructive in her way as he was in his. Sometimes I think people have guiding spirits that lead them to the situations they need. I don't think Jerry knew what he was doing, not consciously. I don't think Dorie knew why she came to Martin's house last week. But their guiding spirits knew all along."

In the candle-lit darkness of that room, with the

balloons bobbing above their portraits of the dead, the portraits bobbing in turn above the ghostly faces of the living, what Martha said seemed realistic and profound. However, my objectivity returned as I saw the front door open and James enter. In a jacket and turtleneck shirt, he looked like a policeman in plain-clothes. Of course, the jacket was required, despite the heat, to conceal his shoulder holster. He saw me at once and saluted. I smiled.

"No, I really believe it," said Martha, misinterpreting my expression. "I really believe all three of them had unhappy guiding spirits. I'm not sure why I say that about Harold. But there was always that touch of cloak-and-dagger about him. I really think he was excited by the *danger* of making pornos. And when we saw him the day he died, he pretended to know a lot about the murders, didn't he, Martin?" I nodded. "He didn't want to come out and *say* it, you understand, but he wanted us to *think* he knew something."

"A fairly good indication of an otherwise empty life," Mr. Bob pronounced.

"Isn't that a bit hasty?" I asked, impatient to make contact with James who was still near the doorway and talking to Empie.

"I don't think so," said Mr. Bob. "You see, Martin, it's possible to learn a great deal about human psychology when working on fan magazines. You get trained to surmise the probable based on known facts. A good fan magazine can be quite prophetic. I'm just applying the same kind of analysis to Harold's behavior that I'd use in concocting a story about him. All things considered, these deaths may have been solutions for the people who died. I think that's the way a lot of us look at it now. Martha here might suggest we let the murderer's 'guiding spirit' take him to his own destiny uninterrupted. After all, what we're really celebrating here tonight are our own lives."

Party talk. It was tempting to continue the conversation. I might have returned to Mr. Bob's point about fan magazine articles being prophetic. I might have suggested another way of looking at it, that some things became prophetic only because they helped create the environment for what they "prophesied." Did Jerome forsee his own death? Or did he just create the environment for it? I was saved from expressing this and from hearing Mr. Bob's counter-theory by James who had completed the amenities to his hostess and had finally threaded his way to me. He took me by the arm and steered me to a quiet corner occupied by Bimbo.

"Holliman was right about you," James admitted with a touch of pride, our friendship happily surpassing any professional jealousy to which he might have been entitled. "They did find one small circle of paper, like confetti, in the car. It matched up. And everything else was right on the button."

"The club?"

"Yes, someone remembered doing it Monday morning."

"The poison?"

"Missing like you said."

"And the taxi?"

"That was a tough one. But, yes, that too. And the stewardess gave us a pretty clear description of the suspect. It's all written down." He handed me his notes.

Bimbo laughed. "Now if you're right about human behavior," he said, referring to something I'd told him earlier, "it should all be wrapped up tonight."

"Tonight?" James was tentative.

"It's okay," Bimbo reassured him. As their dialogue continued, I moved away to study the notes.

When I looked up, I saw that Bimbo and James had apparently reached an agreement, for together they were wending their way toward Empie. They spoke to her briefly. Then she found Boris and together they went about the room, cajoling the guests to grab balloons and to sit on the floor in a circle. All guests in a party spirit, they complied like children eager to compete in games for prizes. When the stage was set, it looked comically eerie—people sitting about in a circle, painted faces suspended above them by winged balloons, all lit from behind by candlelight.

"Friends and lovers," said Boris, entering the circle, "by this time, maybe some of you have forgotten why we're here. Who remembers?" He nodded to Chicken whose hand shot promptly into the air.

"To honor the dead?" she asked.

"I think that's very well put," said Boris. "Are there any other ideas?" There didn't seem to be, and he started to say something when Empie spoke.

"I think it's a little more than to *honor* them," she asserted. "It's that, sure. But it's also to *celebrate* their departures."

"That's beautiful," said Boris. "Very beautiful. Chicken and Empie are both beautiful. We came here to honor *and* to celebrate. Of course, we're used to the honoring, but the celebration idea is kind of new, I mean to our country and century. The closest thing to what we're doing is the Irish wake." He nodded and smiled at James.

"The Irish handled their sorrow in a sensible way, through a kind of celebration of immortality. Few have been so close to their sensibilities since." O'Toole smiled proudly. "Today," Boris continued, "a lot of people *say* they believe in reincarnation or an afterlife. When someone has departed, they *say* it's good because the spirit is one step closer to God or fulfillment. They *say* these things, but their mournful rituals betray their real uncertainty. Well, today we're trying to get back to some basic feelings, back to the basic truth the Irish have understood all along. These balloons," he raised his glass toward them, "are my latest work, kind of a symbol that the so-called 'departed' haven't really left us, but have risen to a higher plane. Let us toast the dear *un*departed, okay?"

A cheer broke out from the guests. The balloons shook, giving one the disconcerting feeling that Jerome, Doris and Harold were nodding vigorously in agreement. Everyone drank. Then Boris gestured to Michael and sat down. Michael started to get up on this pre-arranged cue, but Chicken, apparently moved by emotion, entered the circle first.

Chicken said nothing. She just quietly and methodically removed all her clothing and turned slowly, allowing all sides a generous and complete view. I did not witness all of this, but it was reported to me later. My hand shading my eyes from viewing the spectacle, I did hear a few low murmurs of appreciation, even from those whom I suspected did not ordinarily have a deep appreciation for women. After she had glided off into the candlelight beyond the balloons, I looked up.

A can of beer in one hand and a balloon in the other, Michael entered the circle. "I know most of you didn't know this guy," he nodded to the portrait of Harold suspended from his balloon, "not the way I did. Besides helping me make a lot of money, he was a good and loyal friend. He worked only for me, and he was usually around when you needed him, especially during that bad period of police harassment." He tied the balloon string around the can of beer.

"Harold once asked me, if he ever died, to chug-a-lug a can of beer and toss the empty can into his grave. Well, since he's in the morgue and since Boris tells us Harold's just gone to a higher plane, I'll have to vary the plan." The string now tied around the beer can, he drank the beer almost without swallowing, then let the balloon carry the empty can upwards. "No more police harassment for you, Harold Hauser," he said. "That's one good thing about it." He sat down.

James got up. "I want to assure you I'm not here to harass anybody," he said and then broke into his Irish cop, "but if you're after breakin' the law, I might be knockin' you silly. No harassment, mind you. Don't know how to do that. And all I'll be doing right now is introduce my good friend, and yours, Mr. H. Martin Webb." He grabbed my arm and pulled me up.

Standing there with his arm around my shoulders so that I could not succumb to my natural instinct to escape, he continued, "I should say that this distinguished looking gentleman has many things to distinguish him. Not only is he a close friend of mine these many years, having accompanied me on numerous occasions to seek out and destroy harassment in local pubs, but he has also gained the guarded confidence of a notoriously distrustful Boston police sergeant. And more important even than those two qualifications put together, Mr. Webb *knows* something it would be fitting to reveal on this occasion. Is it the truth I'm telling, Martin?"

I hesitated only a moment, my adrenalin having risen to the occasion. "Yes," I said. "I know who killed Jerome and Doris and Harold. And now I shall tell you."

Chapter XXVIII

Bimbo set up the easel with the large sketch pad. I flipped it to a clean sheet and wrote from my notes.

Page	Subject
10	Martha
18	Doris
24	Georgie
27	Me
52	Empie & Boris
74	Harold
81	Mr. Bob

As I wrote them a light illuminated them, and when I turned I saw that Boris had turned a small spotlight from his painting over the fireplace to me. At first this made the faces around me indistinguishable and helped prevent any stage fright to which I might otherwise have been subject.

"Let's first consider the surviving novel pages," I gestured to my list. "If Jerome wrote these pages to be read, then he may have been showing others how to murder him and was, as an astute policeman observed, inviting death. No one would be better equipped to bring off this seemingly impossible goal. Jerome had a unique talent for assuming the characteristics of others. With his chameleon-like ability, he could communicate probable motives.

"Another, more important, theme which the astute policeman only hinted at may be Jerome's very fascination with the subject of 'getting away with murder.'

"Starting at the bottom of the list, Mr. Bob could get away with murder by assigning an article about a Mafia figure. Someone else would then commit the murder for him. And incidentally, this is not only the last surviving page, but it is probably one of the last pages written. It is page 81 Jerome typed on his own typewriter, and so thoughtfully, on his last afternoon in the Borman Publishing office. This was the only page not punched for a binder. All pages but this one would have been read by the next person on the list, Harold, as is indicated by fingerprints.

"Harold could get away with murder by poisoning his own bourbon.

"Empie and Boris could do it with an accident resulting from two separate art pieces, one ostensibly unaware of the other.

"Georgie could do it with sound, if such a feat is indeed possible.

"But concerning all pages where the theme of 'getting away with murder' appears, it is significant that Jerome was killed by none of the methods he suggested. We may assume from this, at least as a possibility, that other methods were suggested on pages still lost to us. When so many ideas come so close together, there being only five pages between Harold's and Mr. Bob's, then what other imaginative methods might have been suggested on the 24 missing pages between mine and Empie and Boris', or the 22 pages between theirs and Harold's? The mind boggles.

"Who besides Jerome himself would have known about them all?"

"Harold," Georgie blurted out.

"Yes, Georgie," I pointed to him, "Harold who read you your own page over the telephone, Harold whose fingerprints are evident on all but Mr. Bob's page, Harold who died from poisoned bourbon although it was placed in Jerome's bottle and not his own. Harold.

"Who had access to the gun *and* had fingerprints on it *and* would be interested in an old, attractive music manuscript *and* would be likely to hide it at the scene of the crime *and* would be in Boston later *and* had been a burglar before *and* would therefore have thought to look for a concealed key *and* could have gained entrance without one? Harold.

"Who is most likely to have been the man a neighbor saw entering my house? Many facts point to Harold.

"But I know he wasn't in Boston last Thursday," said Georgie.

"How do you know?"

"Well, he was with me. I'm his alibi."

"Yes," I said, bracing myself for betrayal, "because you and he were making a movie that night."

"What?" asked Michael.

Georgie turned sheepishly to Michael. "Nothing very serious," he tried to minimize the offense, "just some loops, some short stag films, nothing you'd want to get involved with." His voice trembled like one unused to confrontation.

"Why?" Michael asked painfully. "Didn't I take care of you guys?"

"Sure you did." Georgie turned to me and pleaded, "Give me a break!"

"It has to come out," I told him.

Georgie breathed deeply, lowered his head and spoke toward the floor. "Harold figured by the time you'd found out, he'd have enough money to go into business for himself. I'm sorry, Michael, but people have to look out for themselves, don't they?"

"I'm just sorry you let that crook lead you astray," said Michael, then mussed Georgie's hair. "Forget it," he said fatalistically, "you're still the best sound man in the business."

"Wow!" Georgie exclaimed. "I don't believe you're taking it like this."

"That's beautiful," said Boris. "That's really beautiful."

"But," I said to Georgie, "you still claim not to know who was there with you."

"I already told you that," he said, "and I was telling the truth."

"What'd you do?" asked Michael. "Keep your eyes closed?"

"That is the story," I said.

"Sounds like him," said Michael.

"At any rate, it doesn't matter," I said, "because we have the film." I nodded to Bimbo who brought the movie projector from the hallway and began to set it up, as I turned the page of the easel pad to serve for a screen. "I know you did not intend it to be this kind of party," I apologized to Empie who was near me, "but it may be useful to look at the film they made that night."

"Aw, please," wailed Georgie, "don't show it. Come on!" He turned to the rest. "Come on! Let's not see the film. I can't stand it. Whoever was there with me, please *tell* the man!"

"I was," said Chicken.

"Were you?" Georgie sighed.

"Wonderful disguise," Chicken complimented him.

"There was another man," I prompted her.

"That was me," said Boris. "I did it as an art piece."

"Was Harold in the film?" I asked.

"No," said Boris. "He was running the camera."

"So much for alibis," I said. "We now see that those originally offered by Chicken and Boris are untrue. Also, why did Michael say Chicken was in his studio when she was not? Why did Empie confirm Boris' false alibi?" I paused, but they were silent. "The reasons are not important. When one is involved in an illegal operation, however artistic, one tends to cover up the comings and goings of another. I would imagine protective falsehoods abound near murder."

"That's so," said Bimbo, putting the projector aside.

"Therefore," I summarized, "alibis can be unreliable. The film would, however, establish new alibis for Chicken, Boris and Georgie if we can be certain that the film we have is the one made last Thursday. And how can we be certain then that Harold was running the camera? We have only the word of three people who have already revealed less than the truth. How do we know they are not still lying?"

"Touché," said Boris.

"What?" asked Chicken.

Before Boris could translate from the French, I went on. "Let's ignore all alibis. And when we do that, then many facts point to Harold. Too many. Exactly *one* too many." I turned to James. The answer was not obvious and would not be readily apparent through simple police procedures. I wondered if he might make the breakthrough Holliman had suggested essential for James to become a superior cop. I wondered if the better cop inside James that Bimbo had sensed might then emerge. But it did not. Not at that moment. He stared at me and shrugged his shoulders.

"It's your lecture, professor," he said.

"That one fact too many," I continued flipping the sketch pad back to the list of novel pages, "is that all these novel pages were postmarked in Boston on Monday, a day when Harold intended to be there but could not be for obvious reasons."

"Someone was trying to frame him?" asked James.

"I agree with you," I encouraged him. "Harold did not commit the murders, although he gave the impression he knew about them."

"That intrigue stuff," said Martha.

"Yes," I said, "but I'm afraid Harold has been grossly misjudged. There have been many instances in this case where we have been similarly erroneous in our interpretation of human behavior. That made it impossible to see into the heart of the murderer.

"For instance, we have to look at Georgie's guilt and know it is real, that he does in fact have something to hide."

"Not any more," said Georgie. "I told about the movie."

"You know I'm not speaking of that. You came to Harold's apartment on Tuesday."

"Sure. You were there. That's no secret."

"The secret," I persisted, "is *why* you came there. You are not the type of person who would risk being associated with a murdered man, not unless it was very important. A package of marijuana would not be important enough. An undeveloped film in which you were so thoroughly disguised *might* be important. But I think you'd gamble on not being recognized. What then would be important enough to risk association with Harold's death? Obviously, something that *would* make that association. I suggest you came to Harold's apartment out of fear."

"Fear... of what?" he stammered.

"Fear that some evidence had been left behind which

would prove you had been with Harold the night he died; your pipe which was not there before and which others have identified as yours."

"I didn't kill him."

"Who did?"

"I don't know. But I didn't. I didn't even pour the bourbon."

"Who did?"

"He did. I saw him pour it himself, and I saw him drinking it."

"But you had none."

"I don't drink!" he protested, holding up his apple juice.

"But you smoke."

"And I left my pipe by mistake. I came back for it. But I didn't kill Harold. He was alive when I left him. He said he wasn't feeling well, so I left him alone."

"We'll accept that," I said, "because it corresponds to your behavior pattern. You wouldn't want to be around during any kind of crisis. If he were going to be ill, you'd want to leave him alone. Yes, we'll accept that and give you a much needed rest." He sighed deeply.

"What about Doris?" I asked. "She, too, has been misjudged. It's easy to do because she is probably the one aspect of the case to which we've all paid the least attention. I myself had succumbed to the assumption that she felt unloved. Her novel page indicates that was also the way Jerome saw her. He was off the mark on that one. Her love life may have been limited, but she *was* loved, and quite intimately." Although I studiously avoided glancing in James' direction during this, I could sense tension from him, and I hastened to add. "It will not be necessary to go into the specifics, for they are not the point.

"Her movements on the day in question are clouded in

mystery. Ordinarily, she had a tryst at what became the scene of the crime, but she did not last Thursday. Up until now, we knew she was going somewhere else, but we did not know where. If we can now assume she went where her automobile went, then where did she go, Bimbo?"

"She came to New York," said Bimbo. "Her car was found on Pier 95. That's where we take the cars that get towed off the street. The police had it all the time."

"Therefore," I summarized, "on the day of the first two murders, Doris' car was driven here, and that evening Doris was discovered dead in Boston. Clearly, the crime involves both cities. Once we accept that, then it becomes possible, considering the approximate hour of death, that Jerome died in New York before he ever got to Boston."

"Uh-uh," said Liza. "Don't think so."

"We saw him," said Mr. Bob. "We looked down from my office window, and we saw him drive off to Boston."

"Well," I said, "let us consider some facts and add a touch of human behavior. In fact," I looked hopefully at James, "since this is a party, a riddle might be appropriate," and I drew one from my dream. "What is the relationship between an anal compulsive person, a cup of tea and a fire hydrant?"*

I hoped James would find the answer, but Georgie responded first. "Didn't Jerry call himself an anal compulsive on my novel page? Everything neat and orderly and so forth?"

"Yes," I said. "It was a reason Jerome wanted to move away from Harold who was quite the opposite."

"A cup of tea," said Empie, "might refer to the special tea I gave Jerry for his weak stomach."

"Yes. Anal compulsive behavior and a weak stomach,

---

*The reader may wish to pause here to consider this question for himself.

they go together to explain the fire hydrant." I paused to see if anyone else would respond, and when no one did, I went on. "We know that Jerome had a very late and very heavy lunch, and he wasn't feeling well that afternoon before he left. He wasn't able to have the tea that usually settled his stomach because he was at the office. Instead, Martha brought him some kind of seltzer drink. Suppose that didn't work for some reason. Remember, he was driving during the rush hour. If he became ill, he wouldn't be able to stop the car. He would have no choice but to keep driving and regurgitate out the window. If he had been on the West Side Highway then," I said remembering my own drive into the city, "I assure you he would have had no choice."

"And the fire hydrant?" asked Liza.

"The probable source of water during these warm nights. Jerome probably drove the car up to an open hydrant and washed the fouled side. He did not know it would distract us from solving his murder more quickly, and he died before he had an opportunity to explain.

"There were traces of poison in his bloodstream, but not a lethal dose. It was the gun that killed him. The gun was fired from above as he probably knelt in pain. The question is who pulled the trigger?

"Harold's fingerprints were on the gun from the last time it had been used in a film. It is doubtful when he took it from Michael's studio that he even removed it from its plastic bag. Why did he take it? Shortly after I met him, he said something about this being a dangerous city in which to live. So he could have taken the gun for his own protection, or for the protection of someone else. Georgie tells us that Harold took it for Jerome. That would explain Jerome's prints being on the gun. However, if we put too much faith in fingerprints, which are as easily manufactured as alibis, then we will begin to think that Doris, whose prints were on the gun, killed Jerome. Then we would be left with the problem of who killed Doris.

"But we haven't finished with Harold yet. Many false assumptions have been made about him, of course. However, one of the most misleading was assuming that because he enjoyed playing games of intrigue he only *pretended* to know something about the murders. He *did* know something, after all. Not only did he know about the gun, but he knew who killed Jerome and Doris. He knew because he had read the page that described the murder as it was committed, the page that was never mailed to anyone."

"Do you mean," asked Mr. Bob, "that the person responsible is someone like Liza, someone who isn't on that list of yours?"

"Not me, Chief," said Liza.

"As you say," I told him, "the person *responsible* does not appear on this list." Sighs of relief were heard throughout the room. "The person responsible is Susan Denham."

"Oh," said Empie, "I'm glad it's nobody here. It would spoil the party."

"Has she been arrested?" asked Mr. Bob.

"No."

"Can't you find her?"

"No, we can't, and we won't."

"Well, why not?"

"There's an important clue in my novel page," I said. "But I'll have to give a little background to those who don't know Shakespeare as Jerome did. In Shakespearean poetry or plays, there are usually five 'feet' in a line, and each foot has two syllables, one accented and one unaccented. In the line 'Oh, what a rogue and peasant slave am I,' there are five metric feet. 'Oh, *what*' is the first, 'a *rogue*' is the second, and so forth.

"Now in my novel page, there is written this cryptic message.

> *Otello, my true love know. There she is,*
> *Unnoticed, Sue of Denham. Hamlet, she's*
> *Like April's pseudo donuts, nymphet for*
> *All my moist dreams. But, come, you too relate.*

When asked what it means, the character responds, 'Just what it says, give or take a syllable.

> *Tap the feet,*
> *Just keep the beat.*'"

"Of course," said Empie. "Jerry became very conscious of words while he was living here because I use words in my art work."

"Rather his interest was intensified here," I suggested. "He has been a word person since I first knew him."

"I still don't get it," said James.

"Do you remember our conversation with Sergeant Holliman when I suggested this case had too many notes and that we had to eliminate the extraneous ones in order to hear the music?"

"Yes," James blinked.

"Well, this is the first movement of that music," I said. "Now consider the directions. We know that in the iambic foot..."

"Tap the *feet*," said James.

"Yes, and in each foot there is one unaccented and one accented syllable."

"Just *keep* the *beat!*" said James.

I was strangely thrilled to see something catching hold in him, some light which illuminated a dark corner of his imagination. He became very excited. I handed him my novel page, and he began to read with exaggerated emphasis on the beat.

> *oTELLo, MY true LOVE know. THERE she IS, unNOticed, SUE of DENham. HAMlet, SHE'S like April's PSEUdo DOnuts, NYMphet FOR all MY moist DREAMS. but COME, you TOO reLATE.*

He laughed, charged with his discovery and read once more, this time only the accented syllables, the beat without the upbeat.

> *"Tell my love there is*
> *no Sue Denham. She's*
> *a pseudonym for*
> *my dreams come too late."*

"In other words," I said, "Susan Denham cannot be found because there is no Susan Denham and there never was."

Then Martha screamed.

Chapter XXIX

Martha's explosion caused a stir which did not subside for several minutes. During that time, she had been seated Indian fashion on the floor in front of me, bent at the waist, not so much in pain as to squeeze the pain out. Empie kneeled down and cradled Martha in her arms.

"I killed him," Martha sobbed.

Instantly, James and Bimbo were beside her. Bimbo told her of her rights to remain silent, to have a lawyer present, and so forth. James was witness to her acknowledgement that she understood. Bimbo rose and grinned at me. "You were right about human behavior," he said, and then he moved back.

"I killed him," she repeated.

"Yes," I said. "You were the only one who claimed not to know anything about the novel.

"Is that how you knew?"

"You were suspicious not because of what was on your novel page, but because of what wasn't on it."

"The way I could murder him." She nodded, sighed and went on. "After all the time I'd given him, after all we meant to each other, I thought he was having an affair with someone else. You're right, Susan Denham was responsible. But I pulled the trigger. Now that I realize it was for nothing, now that I see he maybe did love me, well, I don't care anymore. I don't care what happens to me. I murdered Doris, too. And Harold."

"But not alone."

"Not alone," she said. "Not exactly alone. Doris helped with the first one." She looked up at me. "Did you know that?"

"Yes," I said.

"How?"

"If you recall, shortly after I arrived in this city, you told me you weren't stronger than anyone. It was clear that you would not be strong enough to accomplish Jerome's murder alone. And when I realized that Doris may have been in New York, then I realized the missing auto may have been towed by the police from some street with alternate-side parking. According to police records, her car was towed from your street.

"Although you claim Jerome made a number of calls to Wessex on your telephone, a police check reveals there was a long call on the Wednesday evening before Jerome died, a time when we know he was at home since you brought the car to work for him the next day.

"I wonder," I asked, "is there significance that the two earliest pages were devoted to you and Doris?" I pointed to the list I had made on the sketch pad. "The idea was implanted in your minds, perhaps, before anyone else's, and it had the longest to grow?"

She nodded. "At first, neither of us were really serious about it, we thought; we both believed in Susan Denham, and just planning Jerry's death relieved some of the pain we felt. It had all the relief of sticking pins in a voodoo doll. We just kept each other going until it happened, and I don't think either of us knew when it became real.

"I know, as the planning went on, Doris became more and more dependent on me to work out the details. I realized that our conspiracy bound me as much to her as my love did to him. And that was the last thing I wanted. Afterwards, I wanted to be rid of Doris, to forget that things might have been different for Jerry and me if Doris had gone through with the divorce. I guess I really hated them both very much. She must have hated me, too. And maybe she was planning my death while I was planning hers." She again broke into sobs. "You know it all, don't you?" She asked. "You tell it. I can't."

"I think," said Bimbo, "it's time to remove Miss Simms. Before you say any more," he explained to me. "Wouldn't do to put any ideas in her head that aren't there already." He helped her up and began to lead her away...

"But how will I ever know if I'm correct?" I asked him.

"Want to come along?" he asked.

As I considered the invitation, there was a general protest from the guests, many of them feeling strongly that I should stay to tell my story.

"You must stay," said Empie. "The party wouldn't be complete unless you did. I'll go with Martha."

"Beautiful," Boris agreed. "You've got to stay."

After they had gone, I became suddenly shy and did not know quite where to begin. Georgie produced a pocket tape recorder and proposed to record my version of the story so that all the details could be checked out later. This did not quell my stage fright. Then James put a drink in my hand, and that helped a great deal. The following (with my comments in parentheses) is a transcription of Georgie's tape recording. Let us now turn to that and give my beseiged memory a rest.

WEBB:

Martha reacted as I anticipated. After all, her belief in Susan Denham made the years spent with Jerome seem meaningless. Killing Jerome was a desperate attempt to replace that meaningless situation with a meaningful act. If the act itself turned out to be meaningless, that would be an irony, I felt strongly, which would cause someone like Martha to break down and confess. The substantiation of all facts would then be an academic matter.

As a matter of fact, many of the aspects of this case can only be substantiated through Martha's testimony. All I am able to do in her absence is offer a probable solution subject to verification, but one in which all the parts fit very neatly.

One piece of the puzzle about which I cannot be certain is if framing Harold was the method Jerome suggested to Doris and/or Martha, the method by which either or both of them might get away with murder. I suggest this is probable, however, and that it was an early part of the planning process.

The mailing of the key novel pages was also probably suggested by Jerome. At least, I like to think so because it was an ingenious diversionary tactic. It was more than this, perhaps. It may have been a method for throwing focus on the non-existant Susan Denham, perhaps providing a fictional suspect for his fictional murder.

Martha knew of the novel better than anyone else, since it began some time ago while she was living in Jerome's apartment. She followed its progress as he typed it, and she did not have to touch the pages which were later mailed. She was in an excellent position to plan the mailing, and she had access to the typewriter for typing the envelopes far in advance. The smoother touch with which the envelopes were typed attests to her professional training.

After Martha moved into her own apartment, Jerome brought her the gun which Harold had taken for him. The gun was ostensibly for the protection of a young lady living alone in another part of the city. It was still in its plastic bag when it was delivered. When Martha finally removed it from its container, she was wearing gloves, probably ordinary rubber gloves from her kitchen. I saw her opening a new pair when I visited her apartment, and later it occured to me what might have happened to the old pair. If they didn't wear out, they may have been disposed of along with other artifacts of the murders.

Prior to the murders, there were certain other preparations. Martha ordered a new rug for her apartment. This was quickly established by calling a selection of the most likely department stores. She also persuaded Doris to provide a substantial quantity of poison from the hospital laboratory where Doris worked. A call to the hospital tells us that there is less of the fatal potion in stock than in the inventory.

Another important element of the planning process was timing. When Jerome planned a trip to Boston three days before Harold intended to be there, the time was ripe. Something could be stolen. It could be very old and of little value to indicate Harold's taste as a collector. It could be planted nearby to indicate a former burglar's intent of returning. In addition, the novel pages could be mailed on the day Harold would be in Boston for a personal appearance. I am quite certain that the pages selected for special treatment were those that would suggest Harold was shifting the guilt to Susan Denham. But still the burglary and the intrigue would point to Harold. Later Harold would commit suicide out of remorse, or rather than be executed.

On the Monday when Harold would be in Boston to mail the novel pages, if not to pick up the hidden music manuscript, Doris and Martha would be elsewhere. Doris would be seen at work all day, and she had a liaison planned for that evening. *(I remember James blushed.)* Martha would also be seen at work all day, and that evening she had planned to spend with Empie and Boris. Their alibis would be clearly established on the day the "murderer" was in Boston.

O'TOOLE:

But Harold died before Monday.

WEBB:

Harold's death was controllable by Martha based on her access to the apartment and her knowledge of his drinking habits. By controlling the amount of bourbon in Harold's bottle she could forestall or hasten his drinking from the poisoned bottle.

This brings us to last Thursday.

Martha, Mr. Bob and Jerome go to a late lunch. Jerome eats the wrong foods for his stomach, with Martha's encouragement. In the afternoon, while he types Mr. Bob's novel page, Jerome begins to feel ill, and Martha brings him a seltzer containing a small quantity of poison, not enough to kill him, only enough to be certain he will become quite ill.

He departs as planned around 4:15. At Martha's request on the pretext of something being wrong with the car, Mr. Bob and Liza are conveniently beckoned to the window to see Jerome drive away. As far as they are concerned, he is on his way to Boston.

In the meantime, Doris arrives outside Martha's apartment building. She parks and waits.

Martha finishes work and goes to Jerome's apartment which is empty. She makes certain there is a sufficient amount of bourbon in Harold's bottle to forestall his sampling Jerome's. Then she pours the poison in Jerome's bottle. She probably disposed of the poison bottle, the only object that ever held her fingerprints, by dropping it down the incinerator on her way out, and it was melted or charred beyond recognition before anyone had reason to search for it.

Returning to her own street, Martha settles final details with Doris. Doris is parked on the east end of the one-way street. When Jerome returns, he will enter the street at the west end. Doris is also parked on the side of the street which is a tow-away zone on Tuesday and Friday. It would be safe there until she returned for it later that night.

As Doris watches the street behind her in her rear-view mirror, Martha goes up to her apartment. Once there, she puts some of Jerome's old clothes on over what she is wearing.

Jerome kept two changes of casual clothes in Martha's apartment. Even if she had not told me so, I might have guessed, for Jerome was like that. He believed in just enough and nothing extraneous. The quantity of luggage he brought to Boston shows this characteristic, one typical of whom he himself called an anal compulsive.

When I looked in his drawer on Tuesday, there was only one set of clothes. What happened to the others? Quite likely, Martha wore them.

You can see I am creating some facts, not as an eyewitness, but as an observer of human behavior. Perhaps by knowing how people behave, we can begin to interpret, to know what belongs in a picture and what does not, to be able to detect false notes and be aware of missing notes. Perhaps it all adds up, then, in a particular way, as in a dream.

For instance, it's very likely that Jerome became ill while driving to Boston, but how do we know he would then return to New York? Past behavior—with Empie and with Doris—indicates that when the animal is wounded, he will return to any place he will receive comfort. Jerome will return to Martha's love, not to mention her foolproof tea.

To continue, Doris sees him in her mirror as he turns onto the street at the far corner. She watches him pull up outside the apartment, conscientiously pausing at a fire hydrant to wash traces of his sickness from the side of the car.

Jerome goes upstairs, enters Martha's apartment, perhaps falls over in his weakened state and is shot through the temple by the young lady wearing his clothes and rubber kitchen gloves.

At the sound of the gunshot, as Jerome's blood falls to the rug in the apartment, Doris starts her car which has a tendency to backfire. Thus, the gunshot, which was heard by several people on Martha's street, was interpreted as being the first in a series of tailpipe explosions. Having executed this ploy, Doris turns off the ignition, deposits the keys in her purse and goes upstairs.

To keep the blood contained, Martha wraps Jerome's head tightly in a plastic bag, which also retards clotting and keeps the blood moist. She knew this from assisting Boris and Empie perform their art piece at the Museum of Modern Art where they used butcher's blood preserved in plastic bags.

Doris places the gun back in the plastic bag it came

from, and her fingerprints are never removed from it. Together, Martha and Doris wrap Jerome's body in the rug, which explains identical lint found later on his body and under Doris' fingernail.

Together, the two ladies are able to carry this improbable package downstairs and place it in the car along with the packaged gun, an empty green plastic garbage bag and the pre-addressed envelopes. They start toward Boston where Jerome is scheduled to be murdered by Harold who would attempt to make it look like suicide.

During what must have seemed a strange journey, Doris rips the appropriate manuscript pages from the looseleaf binder and places them in the pre-addressed envelopes. Small, circular bits of paper can cling to punched typing paper and can fall off when pages are ripped from a loose-leaf binder. Search of the BMW disclosed one such bit of paper which matched a punched hole on my own page, when the two were compared under a microscope in the Boston police laboratory.

Arriving in Boston, they stop at a particular athletic club where Doris was once employed. She knows it will be locked and that it will remain so throughout the weekend. She also knows from past experience that any unposted mail will be found and mailed on Monday morning when Harold is scheduled to be in town. They stuff the envelopes under the door and proceed to my apartment.

Once there, they first of all carry inside Jerome's luggage, his manuscript, the plastic bag with the gun and the green plastic garbage bag. On their second trip, they carry the rolled rug. It is about ten oclock, a time when most good working people are watching television or going to bed. But not Mrs. Donahue across the street who saw a man entering my building, either drunk or carrying something. We know now that he was not inebriated, nor was he a man. It was Martha in man's clothing, with her hair up, and struggling with the back end of the rolled up rug. The other end was being held by Doris who was already inside the hallway.

After the body is positioned on the bed, Martha, still wearing the rubber gloves, removes the gun from its plastic bag, ostensibly to plant it near Jerome. Then perhaps as Doris is pointing out the location of my music manuscripts, Martha clubs Doris who falls dead at the foot of the bed.

Jerome's fingerprints are planted on the gun, and the gun is dropped to the floor. The plastic bag is removed from Jerome's head, and the blood inside is scattered in a dramatic way, as Harold might have done it. This plastic bag, along with the one which contained the gun, is deposited with the rug in the large green garbage bag.

Now time is getting short. I could return at any minute. Martha examines the music manuscripts, takes the one she thinks Harold would take and conceals it outside my window as Harold might.

She phones a taxi from my apartment, then leaves the apartment carrying the bag. Mrs. Donahue sees this 'man' emerging. Once out of Mrs. Donahue's sight, the outer clothing is removed, along with the gloves, and these are deposited in a handy garbage can some blocks away. Her taxi meets her at some pre-determined spot and takes her to the airport. A brief canvass of Boston taxi companies reveals an airport pickup near my address. The driver was able to describe Martha and her large purse. Inside the purse was the rest of the novel.

She catches the last shuttle to New York. A stewardess on this flight recalls a girl matching Martha's description reading from a loose-leaf binder. The stewardess particularly noticed that the girl's clothing was wrinkled—probably from having other clothing worn over it—and that she was crying.

Martha is back in her own apartment by 1:00, in time to receive the phone call from the police at 1:30.

Everything happened as planned, save one detail. She forgot to remove the Volkswagen car keys from Doris' body. If it was a mistake, it did not matter, because the next day the car became illegally parked and was towed away to where it would be least likely found, in police custody.

That same day, Martha disposed of the novel in her own garbage can. The new rug arrived and was put down.

Now the scene shifts to Saturday when I accompany Martha to Harold's apartment. Based on Harold's connection with the gun, his love of intrigue and his probable loyalty to Martha, she never expected him to reveal what he knew. Besides the things we have mentioned—the final destination of the gun and the content of the entire novel—Harold may have known something Martha never suspected, that Susan Denham was a product of Jerome's imagination. Had Harold been less secretive, he may have prevented his own murder as well as those of Jerome and Doris.

At any rate, there in the apartment, Martha tested Harold to see if under pressure he would reveal what he knew. By not confronting Martha with his suspicions, he passed the test. But when left alone with me, Harold showed every indication of wanting to tell all. From the bathroom, I discovered, you can hear quite clearly what is transpiring in the living room. From this location, Martha heard Harold trying to tell me secrets and realized she had to act quickly to take me from the scene and to effect Harold's guilt-ridden suicide earlier than planned.

Once again, Martha donned rubber gloves—later found on the bathroom window sill. She reached across the airshaft to the kitchen window sill, took Harold's bourbon, poured it in the handiest receptacle and flushed it away. She replaced the empty bottle, came back to the living room as quickly as she could, extracted me from the apartment with similar haste, leaving Harold to indulge in the only available bourbon at the magic hour of 5:00.

And there you have it.

(Sounds of approval, coughs.)

You know, the only mystery remaining is why I haven't dropped dead myself.

O'TOOLE:

Maybe you thrive on murder, Martin me boy.
(What an absurd idea!)

Chapter XXX

A week later to the day, Dr. Sterne and I were reunited at our favorite table. Prior to this, we had spent some time in our favorite pub. Although I had been afforded a rehearsal earlier with Miss Pinkham, the narration of my tale had still taken quite some time. But I noted that although he had begun the evening somewhat piqued about my absence on the previous Thursday, Dr. Sterne was finally mollified by the tale I have just told you.

"I approve of your concerto analogy," he told me, "but of course it is truly a concerto *grosso*. After all, did not *several* instruments become more important than the balance of the ensemble?"

"True enough," I bowed to him.

"Intentionally or otherwise," he went on, "all these victims participated in major ways in their own deaths."

"Not intentionally, of course. In fact, if Martha could have waited longer, she might indeed have emerged unscathed."

"Why is that?" asked Sterne as the soup course was set before us.

"It has become my theory," I said, "that Jerome created Susan Denham as more than a joke on himself or a symbol of his lost youth."

"Rather extreme, that," Sterne said quietly. "Fantastic even. Putting her name on a mailing list so that circulars would come to his address in her name! After all!" He was outraged.

231

"Yes," I said, "but I have a strong feeling it was Jerome's intent to make Susan Denham the murderer of his novel. Had he finished it before he died, we might be searching for her still."

"Never to be found."

"Never to be found," I nodded. "Only a figment of creative energy invisible to all but its author."

"You might say that he was killed by his own creative energy gone awry." Sterne speculated. "There are a few dangling ends, however," he pointed out. "Did not anyone find the green plastic garbage bag with its damning contents, nor the novel so casually placed in a New York garbage can?"

"Such things," I told him, "are obligingly devoured every twenty-four hours or so by dragon-like machines."

"Barbarian!" he pronounced.

I knew what he meant. Modern barbarian. It was all so modern, this crime, even to the disposal of its artifacts. Portions of death were transported in, of all things, plastic bags, and later disposed of, gone from scrutiny into that kingdom of overlooked and unreclaimable garbage, its pieces torn and crushed beyond recognition and buried without ceremony in municipal graves.

Ancient man had thoughtfully left his garbage heaps for later generations to detect his meaning. But today there was no respect for garbage, and less respect for crime.

Even at the end, there was none of Sterne's respectable outrage. Even the victims had cooperated in the concerto grosso death ritual. Yes, it was truly barbaric.

"What of the principals in the story?" Sterne interrupted my reverie.

"Well," I said, "everyone goes on much as before, except for Martha who has been incarcerated."

"And your policeman friend?"

"James barely returned to uniform before he was promoted to plain-clothes work and took it off again."

"Well," Sterne concluded, "then all ends as it should, at least. Even the soup tonight is excellent. This could be another perfect Thursday for us." His smile froze, and he added gruffly, "I'm sorry."

We were lost in gloom, too embarrassed and fearful to even look at each other. Was this to be the beginning of some fresh disaster? Already, for the first time in weeks, I could feel that uncomfortable feeling in my lungs. Good heavens! Was it to be an attack to embarrass my good friend!?

I tried to get my mind from the spectre that threatened. I busied myself with my soup, he with his. We were lost in our mood for several uncomfortable moments, until a filthy knife from the tray of a passing busboy slid off into my soup, splashing my shirt and tie. I was astonished beyond any other emotion. The Doctor merely smiled.

"At last," he said, "and finally, a good omen."

FINIS

SUSPENSEFUL READING FROM LEISURE BOOKS— GUARANTEED TO KEEP ALL ARMCHAIR DETECTIVES ON THE EDGE OF THEIR SEATS!

2178-1	**MISSING** Susannah Windham	$2.75
2191-9	**THE HAUNTING AT LOST LAKE** Eleana Oliphant	$2.50
2202-8	**A SCENT OF NUTMEG** Colleen Cairns	$2.95
2231-1	**DEATHSTALK** Bruce Clark	$2.50
2241-9	**SENSELESS** J. Douglas Burtt	$2.50
2272-9	**THE OPERA HOUSE MURDERS** David Hanna	$2.75

FOR THE FINEST IN MYSTERY AND SUSPENSE, IT'S LEISURE'S *CRIME COURT SERIES*

2298-2	**MURDER IN WHITE** Hugh Zachary	$2.50
2282-6	**FIVE PORTS TO DANGER** Vivian Connolly	$2.50
5000-5	**WINTER ROSES** Lorinda Hagen	$2.95
5001-3	**MUSIC TO MURDER BY** Vernon Hinkle	$2.95
5002-1	**PRATFALL** T.A. Schock	$2.95

MAKE THE MOST OF YOUR *LEISURE* TIME WITH THESE TIMELY LEISURE NOVELS

1167-8	**SUMMER FRIENDS** Peter McCurtin	$3.50
2040-8	**HEAR THE CHILDREN CRY** Ruby Jean Jensen	$2.95
2162-5	**BALANCE OF POWER** Jack Peterson	$3.95 US, $4.95 Can.
2165-X	**THOROUGHBREDS** Michael Geller	$3.50
2187-0	**THE TOUCH** Patricia Rae	$3.75 US, $4.50 Can.
2197-8	**THE REGULARS** Stephen Lewis	$3.75 US, $4.50 Can.
2267-2	**BEVERLY CENTER** Ryan Woodward	$3.95 US, $4.95 Can.
2277-X	**STRANGERS AND LOVERS** David Drake	$3.95 US, $4.95 Can.
2320-2	**THE COUNTRY CLUB** Nancy Bruff	$3.95 US, $4.50 Can.

MORE ACTION AND ADVENTURE FROM LEISURE BOOKS

1060-7	**THE SCORPIO CIPHER** Ralph Hayes	$3.25
2115-3	**DEADLY REUNION** Ralph Hayes	$3.50
2119-6	**DYED FOR DEATH** Rick Rider	$2.50
2147-1	**ESPIONAGE** William Doxey	$3.50 US, $3.95 Can.
2154-4	**THE TERROR ALLIANCE** Jack D. Hunter	$3.50
2183-8	**THE GOLD SEEKERS** J. Mark Bond	$3.75 US, $4.50 Can.
2210-9	**STOREHOUSES OF THE SNOW** Capt. Ed U. Woodard and Heather Woodard Bischoff	$3.50
2218-5	**DESTROYER** Roy W. West	$3.25
2219-2	**ACTS OF MERCY** Bill Pronzini and Barry N. Malzberg	$2.95
2236-2	**PROJECT JAEL** Aaron Fletcher	$3.95 US, $4.95 Can.
2247-8	**EYE FOR AN EYE** John D. Harris	$3.50 US, $4.25 Can.

EERIE NOVELS OF HORROR AND THE OCCULT BY J. N. WILLIAMSON, THE MASTER OF DARK FANTASY

1168-9	THE RITUAL	$3.25
2074-2	GHOST	$2.95
2133-1	THE OFFSPRING	$3.25
2176-5	PROFITS	$3.25
2228-1	THE TULPA	$2.95

MORE BLOOD-CHILLERS FROM LEISURE BOOKS

2039-4	**LOVE'S UNEARTHLY POWER** Blair Foster	$3.50
2112-9	**SPAWN OF HELL** William Schoell	$3.75 US, $4.50 Can.
2121-8	**UNDERTOW** Drake Douglas	$3.75 US, $4.50 Can.
2152-8	**SISTER SATAN** Dana Reed	$3.75 US, $4.50 Can.
2185-4	**BLOOD OFFERINGS** Robert San Souci	$3.75 US, $4.50 Can.
2195-1	**BRAIN WATCH** Robert W. Walker	$3.50 US, $4.25 Can.
2215-x	**MADONNA** Ed Kelleher and Harriette Vidal	$3.75 US, $4.50 Can.
2220-6	**THE RIVARD HOUSE** Edwin Lambirth	$3.25
2225-7	**UNTO THE ALTAR** John Tigges	$3.75 US, $4.50 Can.
2235-4	**SHIVERS** William Schoell	$3.75 US, $4.50 Can.
2246-X	**DEATHBRINGER** Dana Reed	$3.75 US, $4.50 Can.
2256-7	**CREATURE** Drake Douglas	$3.75 US, $4.50 Can.

Make the Most of Your Leisure Time with
LEISURE BOOKS

Please send me the following titles:

Quantity	Book Number	Price
_____	_____	_____
_____	_____	_____
_____	_____	_____
_____	_____	_____
_____	_____	_____

If out of stock on any of the above titles, please send me the alternate title(s) listed below:

_____	_____	_____
_____	_____	_____
_____	_____	_____
_____	_____	_____

Postage & Handling _____

Total Enclosed $ _____

☐ Please send me a free catalog.

NAME _____
(please print)

ADDRESS _____

CITY _____ STATE _____ ZIP _____

Please include $1.00 shipping and handling for the first book ordered and 25¢ for each book thereafter in the same order. All orders are shipped within approximately 4 weeks via postal service book rate. PAYMENT MUST ACCOMPANY ALL ORDERS.*

*Canadian orders must be paid in US dollars payable through a New York banking facility.

Mail coupon to: **Dorchester Publishing Co., Inc.**
6 East 39 Street, Suite 900
New York, NY 10016
Att: ORDER DEPT.